MW00974686

Undeniable

Higher Elevation Series
Book Three

By Renee Regent

Jaunita
Thanks! The
Enjoy the
Trilogy

Renee Regent

Published by Royal Turtle Publishing

To join the author's mailing list visit http://reneeregent.com

Royal Turtle Publishing
royalturtlepub@gmail.com

Undeniable/Higher Elevation Series/Renee Regent
ISBN 978-0-9981328-5-3

Thanks to all my Atlanta writers for their support over the years. Thanks to Lina Sacher for her editing expertise, and Suzanna Lyons of Funky Book Designs for her awesome cover work. Special thanks to author Josie Kerr for assistance with formatting, and Enticing Journey Book Promotions for promoting my debut series. Thanks to my family for being my biggest fans.

Table of Contents

1   The Message

Where do you go, when you can't go home?
Christian Levine turned the question over in his mind as he neared his exit. The traffic out of San Francisco was getting worse by the day and lately it seemed to affect his entire commute. What should have been a thirty minute drive had already taken over an hour. He glanced again at his watch as his car crept forward. Fifteen minutes, maybe twenty if he missed a light, and he'd be pulling into the parking space assigned to his beautiful, empty condo.

Empty because his ex, Teressa, had taken most of their furniture a few weeks earlier. He'd paid for all of it, and could have insisted she leave everything, but in the end sofas and tables weren't worth fighting over. Better to let her go. That was the moment he'd truly given up—no sense hanging on to a love that had been doomed long ago.

His stomach rumbled, reminding him he'd worked through lunch, and the granola bar and bag of chips stashed in his desk hadn't sustained him. It had been his last day at work, and he'd wanted to wrap up as many loose ends as he could. He'd given the standard two weeks' notice, but his conscience wouldn't let him slack off just because it was his last day. So he pushed himself to make sure the transition would be smooth for whoever took over his position after he was gone.

As he rounded the corner onto his street, he spied a neon sign up ahead proclaiming, "Opa!" He'd passed by the restaurant a million times, and always wanted to try it. Teressa hated Greek food, though, which made it all the more enticing to try it now. He turned into the parking lot, deciding to relax, have a meal and a glass of wine. It wasn't far from the condo and he sure didn't feel like cooking.

As he entered the restaurant, the scent of roasted meat and garlic hit his nose. The place wasn't crowded, being six p.m. on a Monday, but eating alone always felt strange to him so he sat at the bar. Jaunty music from an old man in the corner playing an accordion set the mood, as did the elaborate columns and statues littering the restaurant. It was intimate, dark, and gaudy, but he felt a welcome vibe in the smiles of the employees. A large, curly-haired woman placed a napkin in front of him on the bar.

"Welcome to Tatsou's. You like a drink?"

The woman also placed a menu in front of him, with the name of the place, "Tatsou's Family Restaurant" in gold letters on the front. Everything was gold—the napkins, the tablecloths, the woman's left front tooth.

"Uh, just a glass of merlot, if you have it."

The woman nodded vigorously, dark curls bouncing. "I get you the best. You'll love it."

He let out a long sigh, glad to have a moment to unwind. Teressa had moved out almost a month ago, and here he was, still avoiding going home, and being alone. What was he waiting for? A sign from the universe that it was time to move on?

As if he could trust a divine force in his life. That was the problem with believing, it only helped so much. When he first came to San Francisco fresh out of college with his Bachelor's in Psychology, his dreams were on the verge of coming true. He had won the position of Research Assistant at the Noetics Science Foundation, where he would study the power of the human mind, and also learn how to better utilize his own psychic powers. The Foundation was cutting edge at the time, with a mission to scientifically prove such unexplainable phenomena as telekinesis, astral projection, and remote viewing. For a few years, it went well. But when the founder died suddenly, most of the support and funding was lost and within a year the Foundation was shut down.

He almost felt as lost now as he did then, but not quite. Maybe he was more mature, and could handle it. Or maybe he was just that jaded.

The woman had returned, placing a full glass of ruby-red wine in front of him. "Here ya go, merlot for you. You hungry? You tell Thena what you want to eat."

The menu was extensive, with pages of exotic dishes, so he asked, "What's your special?"

Thena leaned over the bar, her large bosom resting on her arms. "You like Greek food?"

"I think I tried it once in New York. At a diner."

Her eyes brightened. "Why not try sample plate? Comes with gyro, moussaka, spanakopita…"

She rattled off so much food, he nodded, knowing it might feed him for lunch tomorrow if he couldn't finish it all. "Yes, bring that."

Thena slapped the bar. "You got it."

He watched her hustle off to the kitchen, and sipped his wine. The stress of his freeway commute was fading, and he watched the accordion player and the other patrons to pass the time. But it wasn't enough of a distraction to keep his mind off the impending changes in his life. There was no turning back now, he'd finally quit his job to accept a position at his father's consulting firm. The job wasn't what Chris really wanted, and it meant moving back to New York City. But the position of Behavioral Analyst would pay well, much better than what he'd been making as a Research Supervisor. Corporations with several levels of "Yuppie" middle managers and overworked employees were eager for qualified consultants to evaluate, test, and make recommendations for efficiency. Boring work for him, but it would help to solve most of his immediate financial problems.

By the time he finished his wine, Thena was back with a plate of food that smelled heavenly. He ordered another merlot and tasted everything, deciding this would be his new hangout until he left for New York. When the plate was half-empty, she brought him a container and filled it for him. Then she leaned on the bar again, fixing him with a puzzled look. He dabbed his mouth with a napkin thinking he'd missed some sauce on his chin, but she held out her hand, asking, "May I see your palm?"

He held up his right hand, and she took it, turning it so his palm faced up. She peered into it, as if reading a newspaper. He was too amused to be offended, and the meal and wine had made him too relaxed to resist.

"You have an interesting love line...see this, where it branches off then comes back?"

He stared at his palm. "Yes?"

"Someone from your past, a lover...you miss her, no?"

It wasn't Teressa's face that came to mind. It was the one face he could never forget—Sarah's. He didn't answer, so Thena continued, her expression hopeful. "You will find her. And you will find your dream, a new dream."

"I no longer believe in dreams. Sometimes, even when they come true, they turn into nightmares."

She frowned, and continued to examine his hand. "You will change your mind. I see a young person, one who will help you to see what you cannot. You have great power, but have forgotten how to use it."

He considered her words for a moment. In 1978, when he graduated college in Fort Winston, Colorado, he was full of dreams, deeply in love and high on his own potential. Eight years later, he was thirty, alone, and had nothing to show for his years of work, except a few degrees. He'd neglected his psychic abilities and thrown his energy into his jobs and his studies, only to find himself increasingly dissatisfied. The politics of the corporate world and long, grueling commutes had eaten away at his soul. He hadn't changed the world, as he once envisioned; but the world had sure changed him.

Add to all that some bad business investments, Teressa's overspending habits, a few student loans, and it was no wonder he'd lost his mojo.

Thena had released his hand. "Thank you, I'll remember that, Miss Thena."

She beamed her gold-tooth smile at him. "I get you dessert, it's on the house."

He opted to take the baklava home with him, and promised to return. She had earned her tip and he was generous. His mood had brightened, and the empty condo no longer bothered him as he settled in for the night. He was in bed and about to nod off in front of the television, when the phone rang.

"Hello?"

"I'm looking for Chris Levine."

"This is he…" He didn't recognize the deep male voice. *Oh, no. Another bill collector…*

"This is Tad Barclay, calling from Colorado. Your name is on the list of people I need to inform. My son-in-law, Dr. David Engle, has passed away. The family said you were close to him and might like to know."

He almost dropped the phone. *Oh, no. Not David.* Finding his voice after the gut punch of hearing his beloved mentor had died, he blurted out the first thing that came to mind. "How—what happened? He wasn't that old."

The caller's voice wavered. "Heart attack. We were all shocked, it happened so suddenly."

Images of his favorite professor and good friend filled his mind, distracting him for a moment. Recalling his manners, he offered his condolences. "I'm so sorry to hear that. How is his wife doing? And the children?"

They chatted for a few minutes, and he wrote down information about the funeral and the gathering that would be at the family home afterward. When he hung up, he stared at the notepad in his hand. The funeral would be in a few days, in Fort Winston. He immediately regretted having lost touch with David over the years; it had always seemed there would be time to catch up. But the hard, cold truth was that death was undeniable, and no one knew when it might happen.

She might still be there.

He had no way of knowing if Sarah was still in Colorado. Who knew where life had taken her? It had been years since their last contact. She had changed her phone number, and the last few letters he'd sent to her in Denver had gone unanswered. It was clear that after they'd broken it off, she had dismissed him from her life. Could he blame her? They had agreed to go their separate ways, but he knew in his heart now that was a mistake. He'd chosen to follow his career path to California, believing once his dream came true it would solve everything. He thought she'd wait for him, and they would be together forever.

He'd never been more wrong about anything.

Grabbing the phone book, he found the number for the airline, and dialed. "Thank God for credit cards," he muttered, picking up his wallet. He had to get to Fort Winston as soon as possible. The rest of his troubles would have to wait.

~*~

Sarah McKenn made her way back to her desk on shaking legs. She'd done it, and now there was no backing out. Her two weeks' notice was on her boss's desk, and she would soon be on her way to Arizona and a new future for her and her daughter.

Flopping into her chair with a sigh, she glanced over at her co-worker Martina. She was on the phone but raised her dark brows in question, and when Sarah gave her a thumbs up, she returned the gesture. No more talking, no more dreaming. It was time for action. This plan to relocate to Sedona, Arizona had been a sudden decision, but she was ready now to make some long overdue changes in her life.

Sophie was excited, though at five years old, she seemed to be excited about everything. She'd be starting first grade in her new school later that year, which would give them the summer to adjust to desert living. It was a good thing they would have Nadine to show them around and help them get settled. It was Nadine, her ex-boss, who had relocated to Sedona and offered Sarah a position as Assistant Manager at her marketing firm. Tourism was booming there, and with the so-called "Harmonic Convergence" coming the following year, it was projected to explode. Sarah thought it was amazing that anyone believed an alignment of the planets would somehow have an impact on society, but the event was already having an impact on the economy of Sedona, which was a well-known mecca for followers of the New Age movement.

Her new position came with a hefty salary increase and a great benefits package, so she didn't care what brought the tourists in. There was even child care on site at the building where she would be working. She'd be a fool not to take the job, and she had to admit she was looking forward to starting over somewhere new.

But it was the unresolved business she was leaving behind that made her stomach curdle and threatened her resolve to go ahead with her plans.

"Wow," Martina said as she hung up the phone. "You went to Fort Winston, right?"

Sarah didn't stop the filing she was doing. "Class of '78."

"So you probably know that professor who died, Dr. Engle."

Her hand froze over the folder on her desk. *David Engle is dead?* When she found her breath again, she looked over at Martina. "Yes, I knew him. What happened?"

"My friend said he died of a heart attack. I guess he was well known in town."

Scenes flashed in Sarah's mind, of a time she had all but forgotten. It was 1977, her last year at Fort Winston University, and she shuddered at the memory. *Who wants to recall being kidnapped and threatened at gunpoint, then forced to watch your boyfriend taken away by a man who might be a killer?*

It was Dr. Engle who'd unknowingly gotten them into the mess, but he'd also helped to get them out of it. The incident was something she'd worked to forget over the years. She felt sad about his untimely death, but after their ordeal, the man had never been high on her list of people she wanted to spend time with. She also hated funerals, having buried both of her parents.

But Chris might be there.

Christian Levine. The walls she'd built around her heart began to crack at the thought of actually seeing him, in the flesh. Feelings long buried sent up tiny shoots of hope, and she squelched them back down where they belonged. She looked over at Martina, keeping her voice level. It wouldn't make sense to sound excited about a funeral. "That's so sad. I do remember him. When's the funeral?"

"She said it's Thursday. You going?"

Sarah stood up, feeling claustrophobic. "I doubt it. Going out for some lunch. Wanna come?"

Martina declined, and Sarah breathed a sigh of relief as she left the building and headed to her car. It was early May, and the sun was beating down, illuminating the hills in the distance. Fort Winston had been her home for many years, and she'd made some good memories. But there were also reminders of the past, ones she'd rather forget, haunting her at every turn. She hated to leave her friends behind, like Zac and Amanda Daley, who had literally saved her life. But even they understood her need for change, and to provide a better life for her daughter. To find a place they could finally call home.

There was one last anchor weighing on her—the fact she had never told the man who fathered Sophie anything about his daughter. She had never told anyone, not even Zac or Amanda, who he was. Somehow, she'd always believed if she kept it to herself, the secret was hers alone, and so was Sophie.

2   The Dreams

"Mommy, I had that dream again."

The silhouette of her daughter in the half-opened door of her bedroom was the first thing Sarah saw as she opened her eyes. The digital clock on her nightstand read four-thirty-two. "C'mon, honey. Sleep with me."

Sophie bounded up on the bed, snuggling down under the covers. Sarah smoothed the girl's golden hair, which curled at her shoulders. She kissed the tiny forehead and whispered, "Do you want to tell me about it?"

"Yes. At first it was fun, but then I got scared."

Sophie had started having strange dreams recently, and this had become their ritual. In addition to her desire to calm her daughter, she wanted to know the details, since what Sophie described was eerily similar to some of her own past experiences. "What was the fun part?"

"I went outside, in the dark. I saw that white cat from across the street. I called to her, but she ran away. I started chasing her, and I jumped so high, I was almost flying."

She knew Sophie's night time forays were all in her head, and she had not actually left the house. But her dreams usually involved some form of leaving her body and wandering around, seeing and doing things which she would later recount in detail. Like the time she had insisted Zac had a new puppy, describing the creature down to the shape of his ears and the color of his spots. The next morning, Zac, who lived in the duplex apartment attached to theirs, did indeed have a new puppy. He'd found it near their driveway late the previous night. He'd wrapped the tiny thing in his coat to bring it inside, so there was no way Sophie could have seen it, even from the window. Yet she described watching it romp and play in Zac's kitchen. It wasn't conclusive evidence of any sort of power, but the coincidences, and the dreams, kept occurring.

"And what part scared you, Sophie?"

"When I started jumping and flying, I got scared maybe I couldn't come back. Everything was really dark and I felt funny. I started crying and it made me wake up."

"Well, you're here now, and safe. It was just a vivid dream and nothing to be scared of."

As they settled down to sleep, she wondered, not for the first time, if Sophie's strange dreams were an indication of some sort of psychic ability. She wouldn't even be entertaining the thought if she hadn't experienced the incredible power of her own mind, and witnessed strange psychic powers in others. It brought her mind back to Chris, and how they met.

Late in 1977, she was a skeptical journalism student on a hiking trip and looking for a story lead. Rumors of strange phenomena on a nearby mountain had her following a group of kids from the college who claimed to have witnessed everything from UFOs to ghosts to phantom noises and lights. Initially dismissing their tales as drug-induced paranoia, she had her own experience that day which changed her life. She discovered she was able to see things no one else could see, and though she nearly lost her life in the events that followed, she eventually made peace with the fact that not everything in life could be explained.

Like her attraction to Chris. After the incident, she attended a class on meditation in an effort to understand what happened to her on that mountain. He was the class instructor, along with his mentor, Dr. Engle. She recalled the immediate attraction she had felt, the incredible bone-deep pull toward Chris. It had baffled her then and she still didn't understand it. Later she learned he felt it too, when they both realized just how deeply connected they were.

She believed then they were meant to be together. He was staying in Fort Winston after graduation to work at a satellite branch of the Noetic Science Foundation, along with Dr.

Engle. He had even secured a position for her as a Public Relations liaison for the Foundation, and she had been full of ideas and hopes for the future.

But right after graduation, it all fell apart.

Sarah shifted in the bed, her legs jittery. Her jaw clenched with the memory of that horrible summer. She turned over and punched her pillow. Sophie's soft breathing calmed her, and her thoughts returned to the past.

She had just moved in to Chris's apartment, when her mother called with bad news. Her doctors had found cancer in her lungs, and treatment was to begin immediately. They gave her six months to a year to live. Sarah was devastated, and though Chris tried to comfort her, she knew what she had to do. Being an only child and her mother a widow, she had to move back home to Denver to care for her. Chris helped her move, but as soon as he returned to Fort Winston he called her with more bad news.

"Dr. Engle is off the project. He's taking a position at the request of the government, to help with a program for rehabilitating MK-Ultra victims. They are trying to mitigate some of the bad press they've gotten over the whole thing. Secretly testing and torturing people, messing with their minds, not to mention the lives they've ruined…it's going to take some work to rectify."

"Wow. Is the Foundation still going to let you work there, in Fort Winston?"

"Uh, I'm afraid not, Sweet. The whole idea has been scrapped. I guess they didn't get the funding they'd hoped for, and without Dr. Engle…well, they still want me to work for them, though. In California."

She still felt the ice that had seeped into her veins during their phone call. There was no way she could leave and go with him. She certainly couldn't ask him to stay, to give up on his dream. It was something he had been working toward long before they met. "That's great they still want you. I'm happy for you. But not for us."

He apologized, though she told him there was nothing to apologize for. They would have to take it one step at a time. He agreed, and they spent another night together before he left for California, but it was bittersweet. The soul-deep connection they had was still strong, which made it more painful when they parted.

Long distance love wasn't the same as being together. A few phone calls, followed by a letter or two. Eventually the stress of dealing with her mother's illness and putting her career on hold took its toll, and soon she found she didn't have the strength to hold on to a love that was fading away.

Sarah stared out the window at the silver-white wedge of a half-moon. Had she been wrong to let him go? Chris told her he loved her in those calls and letters, but he wasn't there. He wasn't by her side all those nights she spent at the hospital, or the days at home when her mother was too weak to even make it to the bathroom unaided. He wasn't there to help cook dinner, or rub her aching feet after her shift at the hardware store, a job she took just to make ends meet. She'd given up on her dream of being a journalist, which would likely involve long hours and travel. Her top priority then had been making sure her mother was as comfortable as possible, so she made peace with putting her own life on hold. She had no time or energy for socializing, or hanging on to a relationship that was doomed by time and distance.

The last time they talked, on New Year's Day 1979, she told him it was over. He was upset at first, and though neither of them really wanted to break up, that's what they did. It wasn't fair to either of them to hang on indefinitely. Afterward, the she disconnected the phone because they were behind on bills, and she threw Chris's letters in a drawer, unopened. It was all too painful, and she only wanted to forget him so she could focus on survival.

"A thousand miles and eight years. That's a long damn time, and way too much distance."

She'd whispered the words, trying to convince herself that even if Chris came to town for the funeral, was there any point in seeing him? He'd moved on with his life, she'd seen to that by ignoring his letters. Maybe she was better off without him. She had Sophie to worry about now, and a new life ahead of her. It was not the time to be chasing after the broken dreams of the past.

A dream that turned into a nightmare.

She sighed and snuggled into her pillow. She'd deal with it all tomorrow.

~*~

It felt weird to be back in Fort Winston. It was the day before the funeral, and he was pacing his hotel room. He'd long ago lost touch with any friends he'd had from college, and going to Dr. Engle's family home seemed intrusive. He'd pay his respects to the family tomorrow at the funeral and the wake, which was really just a gathering of mourners and would be held at the Engle home after the burial. The tension, and hopefully the level of awkwardness he felt, might be less by then.

He'd taken a drive around town earlier past the old college campus, which still looked the same. The kids, hanging out in groups, seemed so young. In his mind, those days felt like yesterday, but a look in the mirror told him he wasn't a kid any longer. He didn't look like a hippie any longer, either. His face was clean shaven now, his hair feathered and cut to just above the collar. He looked the part of a professional, even though he sometimes longed for the freedom of his youth, to look and behave as his mood suited him. Though he had resigned himself to the responsibilities of adulthood, a rebellious streak still remained, buried deep inside.

It was that feeling now, urging him to be daring, and to try to find Sarah. He looked in the phone book, but didn't see her name. He never even got the chance to console her after her mother died—had she died? It seemed inevitable, given the situation. It irritated him now that Sarah had so completely cut him out of her life. They had broken up, but he still cared what happened to her. If he did see her tomorrow, would she even speak to him?

If she rebuffed him again, that would be the end of it. Which would be a shame—he'd never had the connection with anyone else that he shared with Sarah. No one came close to understanding him the way she did. They had a history; she knew all about his ability to astral project, hell, she was the only one who'd ever been able to see him doing it, and to actually do it with him. The sex they had was beyond incredible, physical and mental and psychic all at once. He'd had great lovers since then, but nothing came close to the experiences they shared. *Would it be the same, now? Could we make love like that again, after all this time?*

The thought was tempting and made him more eager to see her. He decided to take a drive by his old apartment on Remington Street, just for nostalgia's sake. Then he'd have dinner at the old diner next to the motel where he first met Sarah. They'd met in that motel when she attended the meditation class he'd been teaching, and he wished he could go back to that moment, knowing what he knew now. But that was only a wish. If he didn't get the chance to see her again, let alone have another try at a relationship, then at least he'd have great memories of a time when they were together.

He picked up his key and headed out the door. It wouldn't hurt to wallow in the past, just for an evening.

3   The Wake

Sarah had just enough time the next morning to get Sophie fed and dressed. She'd gotten up on time, but both of them seemed to be moving in slow motion after a restless night of interrupted sleep. She was grateful she only had to take Sophie next door to spend the day with Amanda, who met them at the door with a cheerful smile.

"Good morning, you two. There's my reading buddy." She picked Sophie up, settling her on her hip. The child nestled in on her shoulder and Sarah's heart melted just a bit, knowing she would miss this woman who had become a friend and confidant, not to mention that Sophie idolized her.

"She's getting heavy, Mandy. You've enough to carry lately, haven't you?"

Sarah gestured to the roundness of Amanda's belly, her oversize t-shirt taut enough to show the bump of her navel. The baby, her first, was due in a month or so. *Another reason to feel guilty for leaving...*

The red-haired woman laughed, a blush creeping onto her freckled cheeks. "Oh, don't worry, I come from sturdy stock. But Sophie is growing fast. Such a smart, big girl." She set her down, then asked, "Do you know which book you want to read today? I brought home some new ones from the library. They're on the coffee table."

Sophie's face lit up, and she hurried to inspect the new books. Amanda worked part-time at the local library and occasionally as a substitute elementary school teacher, so Sarah couldn't have found a better person to watch her daughter. Plus, she just plain loved her best friend's wife. "Zac off to work already? Haven't seen him at the office lately."

Amanda walked to the kitchen. "He's off on a photo shoot this morning. Coffee?"

Her nerves were already jittery, which was ludicrous. "No thanks. Had some already. I should be home by four or so. I'm not going to the funeral, just the gathering afterward. I doubt the wake will take that long. Just going to pay my respects."

Amanda's copper-brown eyes flashed and she raised an eyebrow. "So you decided to go after all? Good for you."

"It's not a big deal. There probably won't be anyone I know there. And if there is, well...it's been a long time."

"Then why are you so nervous?"

There was subtle amusement on her friend's face. Zac had long ago told his wife the tale of their adventures in college that stemmed from Sarah's involvement with Chris Levine. It was years later, after a few bottles of wine, that Sarah confided in her friends just how involved she had been with the man she had believed was the love of her life.

So what is he now? Just a guy I knew?

"I don't know. There's a lot left unsaid. And I'm not sure whether or not it should stay that way."

Amanda touched her arm. "Do you still have feelings for him?"

"I honestly don't know what I feel. I gave up thinking about the past. Since I gave my notice at work, I'm just ready to get on with my life. Dealing with long-lost lovers from the past seems like asking for trouble." She hadn't even formed the thought until she said it. That's what was making her so uneasy—the idea that something or someone might get in the way of her plans to leave for Arizona.

"Well, don't overthink it. If you're sure it's the right thing to do, nothing will stop you. Though, you know we'll miss you horribly."

She hugged Amanda, fighting the lump in her throat. "We'll miss you guys, too. That's my only regret so far. And not being here for the baby's arrival." She patted her friend's protruding tummy, then settled her purse on her shoulder. "Bye, Sophie. Mamma's leaving for work now."

After hugs from her daughter and Amanda, she got in her car, grateful for the twenty minute drive across town. It would give her time to think. She'd work half a day, run some errands, and then attend the wake at the Engle family home. She'd opted not to attend the service or burial, as it was too much for her to handle emotionally, and she wasn't all that close to Dr. Engle.

So, if Chris wasn't there, that would be the end of it. If he was, she'd just be polite. What happened long ago was water under the bridge. They'd gone their separate ways, and had their own lives to live. Even if he was interested in her, there was no way he'd follow her to Arizona. He probably had a family anyway, and his big-time career as a Psychologist of some sort in California. To speculate on anything else happening was a waste of time. She was no longer a wide-eyed college student, and had no time for romance, psychic or otherwise.

A shiver came over her, followed by an unexpected rush of desire. Shocked at her body's quick reaction, she pushed the mental image of Chris, naked and beneath her, from her mind. Their lovemaking had been exquisite, unusual, and sometimes frightening. He had been able to astral project his mind out of his body, and she was the only person who could see him do this, at least back then. They had made love not only physically, but spiritually, and psychically. It was unexplainable then, and likely always would be. She'd had other lovers over the years, and some were damn good. But no one came close to making her feel what she felt with Christian Levine.

Wouldn't it be crazy if it still worked like that? If we still had it…

"So what? What would that prove?" She muttered aloud, banging her hand on the steering wheel. She was pulling into the lot, and it was time to get to work. She was training Martina on some of her duties today, and could not afford to lose focus. Sexual fantasies were especially off-limits.

As she walked from the car to her office, she smoothed the skirt of her dress. It was the only black one she had, and the neckline was a bit risqué for the office, but a blue cotton sweater over top made it respectable. Her legs were bare, but her strappy black sandals looked dressy. Then there was the silky, lacy bra and panties she wore, her best set, which made her feel just a little embarrassed. No one else would know, but some part of her wanted to be prepared, just in case.

In case of what, McKenn?

She had no answer for her conscience, and walked through the doors, all business on the outside, a trembling pile of desire and conflicting emotions on the inside.

~*~

Chris drove to the Engle family's house on the edge of the park, recalling the way as if he'd just been there yesterday. The funeral service and burial had been somber and tedious. Still, it was comforting to hear others speak of Dr. David Engle and his accomplishments. He'd always looked up to the man, and apparently many others had as well. It was standing room only at the service, and Chris found he did see a few familiar faces, guys he went to classes with at Fort Winston University.

But there was one face missing, and it was the one he'd traveled across three states to see. Sarah hadn't shown, which meant she was likely living somewhere else. With someone else. He felt a fool for even hoping to see her again, and an even bigger fool for entertaining the hope of rekindling their romance. *Just to touch her one last time...*

He'd decided to go on to the wake, since he had nothing else to do with his time. He'd spoken to Celia, David's widow, at the memorial service, and she held onto his hand for a moment. She talked of how David had such high hopes for him, and he thanked her for remembering. But it only increased his feelings of falling short of his aspirations. He decided he was glad in a strange way that his mentor would never know what had become of Chris Levine.

He parked a block down the street and walked to the house. Cars were everywhere, and clusters of people were on the sidewalk, in the yard, on the porch. He entered the house to find more people, and a table in the dining room laden with food. There was a beverage table with everything from lemonade to soda pop to bourbon and wine. He spiked his cola with bourbon, just to take the edge off, and munched on a piece of cheese. The mood in the house was quiet, but with an undercurrent of relief. This is what wakes were for, to ease the transition of those left behind from grief to acceptance. He wandered through the rooms, and ended up on the edge of a group that was discussing the good old days at FWU.

He'd just finished his drink and was contemplating another, when he saw her. Her long brown hair was in loose curls streaked with gold, but the face was the same. Moss-green eyes, wholesome looking cheeks, and lips he knew tasted like honey. He stood frozen, watching her make her way into the living room, and a shiver came over him. It was as though his skin was tingling from the urge to touch her. His heart had sped up and he took a long breath to calm himself.

Sarah was there, right in front of him, and she seemed to be alone. It was now or never. He took a step, and then stopped when a tall, blond guy folded her in a bear hug.

Sarah's breath hitched in her throat as Wes Porter swept her up into a hug. *God dammit. Crap. I knew I should have skipped this...*

He was a good six inches taller than her, and his breath reeked of alcohol. Her mind flashed back to a night, to a memory she'd worked hard to forget. She pushed on his chest and he let her go, but didn't back up. She was against a wall, trapped.

"Man, Sarah, it's so good to see you. What's it been...five years?"

"Six, and not long enough, actually, Wes. Now, if you'll excuse me-"

"Oh no. We have some catching up to do. Let me get you a drink."

Thinking he'd go to get her drink, and she'd have time to escape, she gave in. "Uh, sure. I could use a soda."

He slugged down the rest of what was in his cup, and leaned in close to her. His watery blue eyes seemed unfocused, and his grin was more of a leer. Still, he was a handsome guy, who'd always seemed to have no problem finding dates, which made it even more of a puzzle why he always seemed to have a crush on her. She had no romantic interest in him back in school, and certainly had none now.

His voice low, he spoke next to her ear. "You look even sexier than before. I never could forget you."

Her stomach clenched, and she wanted to slug him but thought better of it. It would be disrespectful to make a scene, and she had just arrived. But she wasn't going to let him get any further. "Well you should. I'm leaving the state in a few weeks."

"What? No way. Well, we should go out, then. Give you a hell of a good time before you leave."

He bent down as if to kiss her, and she turned her head away by instinct. She felt a sloppy kiss on her cheek and she pushed on his chest again, but he tightened his embrace. She no sooner said the word, "No" when Wes was shoved away from her, and stumbled back, nearly knocking over a lamp.

"Leave the lady alone."

If she was surprised a moment ago, she was in shock now. Her rescuer was familiar, the husky voice, the broad set of his shoulders. His hair was neatly trimmed and his face clean shaven, but the sapphire blue eyes she knew so well were fixed on Wes Porter with an ominous glare. Her heart was beating so frantically in her chest it scared her. She gulped as the two men faced each other, and the entire room watched in awe.

He's here. For real.

Wes stood slowly, his face growing red. He pulled himself up to his full height, and stared at Chris. Then he smiled, his fake, charming grin she knew he used like a mechanic uses a tool. "If that's what the lady wants, then I guess I will. But she knows what she's missing."

With that, Wes sauntered off, greeting people as he went, unruffled. Sarah breathed a sigh of relief, then looked at Chris. Still stunned, she opened her mouth to speak, but nothing came to mind.

"Are you okay?" His hand touched her arm and she felt a tingle, like a static electricity spark, which turned into warmth that spread through her. *Oh, wow. Just like the first time...*

"Yes," she managed. "Thank you. I can't believe...I didn't expect..."

He was saying much the same thing, speaking in fragments, so they both laughed. His laugh was a sound she thought she'd never hear again. He moved forward, and drew her into a loose hug. Waves of vibrations cascaded over her, and she pulled away. He must have felt it, too, the surprise evident on his face. She just stared, amazed that he could be even more handsome than ever, his face unobscured by the moustache he wore back in the 'seventies. She'd never seen him in a suit before, either.

"You clean up nice, Mr. Levine. So how's California?"

~*~

He thanked the universe silently for bringing him the gift of Sarah once again. He'd have gladly fought a roomful of big blond guys for the chance to be with her like this, talking and laughing. She was even more gorgeous now, not as thin, but with the curves of a woman. She was dressed up, but he was sure she'd be sexy as hell in a pair of jeans and an old tee shirt, too. Though it was clear she'd been rattled by the guy who'd tried to maul her, she was self-assured and in control. But a part of him knew he could still make her lose control in the most delicious ways.

He brought her a drink and they sat in a corner, catching up. He'd told her the bare minimum, about the mess with the Foundation, and his subsequent jobs. He refrained from telling her about New York and his future, and he wasn't sure why. "Enough about me. Did you come up from Denver today, Sarah?"

"No, I live here in Fort Winston. With Zac."

He couldn't stop his frown at the recognition of the name of her best friend from college. Not his biggest fan, Zac had been protective of Sarah and had never seemed friendly. She shook her head and continued, "Not with him, actually. He's married, to Amanda, remember her? Anyway, Sophie and I live on the other side of their duplex."

"Oh." Tension left his face and he felt some hope. "Is Sophie your roommate?"

She looked down, and licked her lips, hesitating. Then with a challenge in her eyes, explained, "No, Sophie is my daughter."

A thousand questions popped into his head, but he ignored them. *A daughter? Interesting.* "That's great. Sounds like you've been busy."

She winced, and he knew his words smacked of sarcasm, which he hadn't meant. He was taken by surprise just seeing her; finding out she was someone's mother threw him off even more. She excused herself to the restroom, and he stood there, berating himself for his awkwardness. He was thirty years old, not an inexperienced kid. He should know how to talk to a woman.

But she's not just any woman, is she?

On her way back, she stopped to talk to Celia, ending their conversation in a hug. When she returned to his side, he could tell she was ready to leave. His window was closing, and he had to do something.

"I have to get going, but it was so great seeing you, Chris." Her smile was bright, but there was a sadness in her eyes. He knew his own eyes must reflect the panic he felt at the thought of never seeing her again. "I can't tell you how glad I am you're here. But I'm staying in town through the weekend. Have dinner with me?"

Her mouth twisted in contemplation, but her eyes showed she was tempted. "I don't know. I have a lot to do. I'm moving in a few weeks, I have work, and Sophie…"

Don't let her go. "Well, how about lunch tomorrow, then? I'll pick you up at work."

She agreed, and gave him the directions. As he turned to walk her out, he looked over his shoulder to find the big blond guy within earshot, still grinning at him. He had a feeling their altercation was far from over.

She'd snagged a parking spot across the street, so he walked her to her car. They hugged again, this time with full body contact and he felt his head swim for a moment. She'd always had the power to knock him off kilter and apparently still did. He stood in the road and watched her car disappear down the street, and he felt like dancing right there, in full view of everyone at the wake.

4 The Deflection

Sarah's head was spinning. Her mind was a jumbled mess of images, and she didn't know what to focus on first. She really hadn't believed Chris would be there, so she was unprepared for the avalanche of feelings the encounter had unleashed. Along with outrageous desire, because he looked so freaking hot, and the comfort of him rescuing her from Wes, was the long-buried hurt she still felt from his abandonment.

The traffic was sluggish, and as she waited at a light, she turned on the radio. Boy George was singing about being hurt, and though she knew Chris had never meant to hurt her, it didn't change how she felt. When they broke up, she had been the first one to let go, but at the time she felt there was no other choice. But if he had made it a point to come after her, to break through her self-imposed walls, maybe things would have turned out differently. The fact he'd stayed in California still stung her, though she knew in her heart is was unreasonable to expect otherwise.

"But that's too much to ask isn't it? He had a career to pursue."

Talking to herself helped, though she hoped the other drivers didn't see. She sang along with Boy George for a few minutes, and it seemed to calm her nerves. There would be time to sort out her feelings about Chris later, after Sophie went to sleep. But the image of her daughter's face brought to mind her other problem.

As surprised as she was to see Chris, she was utterly unprepared for the shock of seeing Wes Porter. As far as she knew, he still lived in Denver at his family's estate when he wasn't traveling the world. She'd lost track of him after their last encounter, and she had hoped to keep it that way.

My biggest mistake…and my greatest blessing.

Memories flashed like a movie trailer in her mind, replaying those dark days late in 1979, just after she'd buried her mother. Numb with grief, she had accepted the invitation of some well-meaning girlfriends to go out for a night on the town. They'd hoped to cheer her by dining at a fancy restaurant and then going dancing. She found the distraction helped, and by the time they reached the club she was actually smiling. The consumption of a few margaritas followed, and her anger over the unfairness of her situation rose to the surface. She found herself out on the dance floor, working out her frustrations by moving to the pounding beat.

That's when Wes appeared. Tall, blond, handsome and rich. She had always avoided his advances before, but now she thought, what the hell? He smiled just for her, and she even noticed a few girls looking their way with envy. *I deserve a little fun, after what I've been through.*

Wes focused his pretty-boy smile on her, and his attention felt nice. It had been so long since she'd been with anyone. He knew how to dance and took control, moving closer and closer. Soon they were kissing on the dance floor and the rest of the world spun away.

It was as though she was on auto-pilot for the rest of the night. Thinking and feeling took too much effort, caused too much pain. It was easier to go along for the ride, wherever it took her, than to deal with reality. They ended up parked on a hill overlooking the city, having sex in the backseat of his BMW. It was awkward, and though he made an effort to please her, in her inebriated state she was just going through the motions.

Reality had smacked her sideways then, bringing her back to her senses too late. She had the good sense to insist he wear a condom, because she'd gone off the pill while caring for her mother. Her own health needs had been put aside, and she figured she wasn't dating anyway. But when he finally groaned his release and pulled away, she knew something was wrong. There was a wetness she knew she shouldn't feel; she hadn't been that turned on. Wes threw the used condom out the window, and moved to the front seat. She scrambled to put her clothes back on, hot tears of shame welling up in her eyes.

What the hell have I done?

The images faded away like snow melting in the sun. She gripped the steering wheel tight, inching forward as the traffic merged. It had been years since she thought of that night. She'd moved on with her life since then, and she had to say she'd been happy. Having Sophie was the best thing that had ever happened to her, though being a single mother wasn't easy. But she'd never told Sophie, or anyone else, who her father was.

And she'd never told Wes Porter he had a daughter.

~*~

Laying back against the pillows, Chris sipped at his wine. The dinner from room service had filled him up, but he still felt an emptiness. Seeing Sarah had been wonderful and awful, all at the same time, and it left him uneasy.

Mrs. Engle had given Chris an envelope at the wake, and he picked it up, spilling the contents onto the bed. In it were notes on the work they'd done long ago, as a result of their encounter with an old friend of Dr. Engle's, who turned out to be a spy for the Russians. It was a crazy time, and all but forgotten. Chris set the notes aside, hoping there might be some information he could actually use.

There were photos, most of Chris and Dr. Engle, but a few had Sarah in them. One was taken at an afternoon cookout at David's house at the beginning of the summer of 1978, just before everything changed and their relationship fell apart. She was smiling, not a care in the world. So different from the smile she had today, with a trace of sadness around the edges. He couldn't help but wonder if some of that was his fault. He had left on a grand quest for this career that was supposed to help him change the world, but that never happened.

If he had stayed, would he still be with Sarah? He had a million questions for her, but he would have to take it slow, or risk scaring her off. The problem was, he didn't have much time.

The phone on the desk rang, jarring him out of his nostalgic trance. "Hello?"

"This is the front desk, Sir. I have a message from a Mr. Levine, who called earlier while you were out. He would like you to return his call."

He jotted down the number on a notepad. He'd left a message with his mother that he'd be in Colorado for a few days. The job he'd accepted didn't start for a few weeks, so he didn't think his father would care much about his unexpected trip. Still, he dialed the number and braced himself.

As expected, Joachim was short on small talk, getting straight to the point. "Chris, when I offered you this position, it was in good faith. I expected my eldest son would be honest with me."

A sinking feeling came over him, but he kept his tone light. "Dad, I have been. What's this about?"

"You know I'm only one of several partners in this consulting firm. I may own several companies, but still have to adhere to protocol when it comes to joint projects. Even though you're family, we still had to run a credit check on you, and it came back with some…well, it wasn't what I expected of you."

Crap. What now? "I meant to tell you I'd had some…issues lately, but I didn't think it'd matter. I've got the condo on the market and when it sells, I can get caught up."

They went back and forth, Chris trying to explain without divulging the details. Throwing Teressa under the bus wouldn't help his case, and the money she'd spent was long gone. He'd just have to figure it all out somehow. At the end of the conversation, he'd convinced his father it was all a misunderstanding, and he'd have his credit repaired in no time. "Once I'm there and they see what I can do, they'll forget all this. You know I'm responsible. I've just had a few bad breaks recently."

"I'll do my best to smooth this out, son. But it would help if you can get here as soon as possible, though. A few of my partners still have their own candidates in mind, and it would show them you're serious and ready to begin working."

"Well, I understand that, but…"

"But what?" His father's voice held an edge, which made him cringe.

"I may need to extend my stay here in Colorado, for a few days. Some unfinished business."

The silence on the line was almost worse than being lectured. He promised to keep his father informed and ended the conversation before he got in any deeper.

When he hung up the phone, he realized what he'd just done. This time, he'd put his career on hold for a tiny chance to make things right with Sarah McKenn.

He hoped he wouldn't come to regret it.

~*~

The alluring scent of pot roast greeted Sarah as she entered Amanda's apartment. In the living room the television was blaring, Zac was strumming an acoustic guitar, and Sophie was giggling and playing with the puppy, a brown and white mutt who was now twice the size he'd been when he joined the family.

"Look, Mommy! I taught Frodo to fetch."

Sophie threw a chew toy across the room, and the puppy yipped and went to retrieve it. He brought the slobber-laden thing back to Sophie and spit it out, tail wagging. Sarah winced as her daughter picked up the toy, and tossed it again. "That's great, honey. Now go wash your hands, we need to get home."

Amanda looked up from the table, where she was setting out plates. "No way. You're eating dinner with us. It's almost ready."

Her grin was friendly but her voice firm, and Sarah was worn out anyway. "Okay. But this time, I do the dishes."

"Whew!" Zac called from the sofa. "I was afraid I'd have to do the cleanup. Thanks, McKenn."

She gave him a sneer, but he chuckled and went back to his song. Her heart tugged a little at the warm family scene, and the fact she was no longer going to be a part of it. Amanda handed her a glass of iced tea and said, "Sit. Tell me what happened at the wake."

A long sip bought her a moment to regroup, then she decided to be bold. "He was there, and we talked. He still lives in California, but said he'd be here through the weekend. We're having lunch tomorrow."

The music stopped, and Zac walked past them to get a glass. "Lunch with who?"

"Chris Levine. He came in for the funeral."

"Ahh."

It was one word, but his tone spoke volumes. Chris hadn't been his favorite person, but Sarah knew Zac was biased when it came to her. When she and Chris were dating, there hadn't been much time for the two men to get to know each other. But none of that mattered now, since it would all be over in a few days. "It's just a lunch. We'll catch up, talk about old times, and go our separate ways. Simple as that."

Pouring tea into his glass, he didn't look at her but nodded. "Hmm. Sounds like a good plan." He placed his glass on the table and went to take the dog outside, and Sophie wandered off to the bathroom to wash.

Amanda nudged her arm. "So how'd he look? Was he nice?"

"Yes, he was charming, as always. He looked great, no longer has a moustache. Kinda yuppie-ish." She refrained from mentioning how he rescued her from Wes, which would only invite more questions.

"Cool. So you have a last fling before you go off to Arizona." She winked, and started filling plates.

Sarah rose to help, getting a loaf of bread from the counter. "Oh, nothing like that. I'm still kind of mad at him for leaving, the first time. Though I know it's probably not fair, since we both agreed to part. But still…"

"You know how guys are, they don't think the way we do. If you don't tell them how you feel and expect them to guess, you'll have a mighty long wait. That's what my Mom always said, anyway."

Sarah smiled. She had met Amanda's mother, Peggy, a few times. Her feisty nature and outspoken opinions were usually amusing, though she couldn't imagine she was always easy to live with. "Well, that's probably true. But it really doesn't matter. He'll be gone soon."

An hour later, she and Sophie were home and in their pajamas. Playing with her dolls, Sophie acted out whatever story she had in her head, while Sarah went through the hall closet, preparing for the move. Keeping her hands busy with a mundane task helped her to think, and she had plenty to think about.

Have I been unfair to Chris, holding a grudge all these years? Was he just being a clueless guy, or did he really not care what I was going through?

"…and baby makes three. Now, they kiss…"

She looked over at Sophie, who had her Barbie and Ken dolls in some kind of awkward embrace, their unbending arms at odd angles. She was making loud smacking sounds and giggling.

"Honey, what are you playing?"

Blue eyes the color of faded denim looked up at her, then back at the dolls. "Barbie and Ken got married. Now they're having a baby, like Auntie Amanda and Uncle Zac."

Sarah leaned down. This sounded serious. It was natural the baby coming would spark the girl's curiosity, but they hadn't discussed it yet. "Well, that's nice. I wish we could stay and meet the baby when it comes, but we'll be in Arizona by then."

"Oh. Can we have a baby of our own, then?"

She ruffled her daughter's blonde curls. "Maybe someday. Have to find a daddy first." She turned back to the closet, determined to finish the job. A small voice behind her said, "Where's my daddy?"

Frozen, she stared at the stacks of towels. She'd put off discussing anything to do with the identity of Sophie's father, but the girl had finally begun to question it. She'd known this moment would come, but she wasn't ready to deal with it just yet.

"We haven't had dessert, have we? I think there's some mint chip ice cream in the freezer."

Sophie's delighted squeal told her the deflection worked. For now.

5   The Invitation

Chris had gone all-out, spending the morning at the local butcher, bakery, and gourmet food shops in downtown Fort Winston. Knowing she had to return to work, he stopped short of picking up a bottle of champagne, opting for sparkling cider instead. He snuck out a blanket from the hotel and by the time he met Sarah in the parking lot of her office, he had the makings of The Most Romantic Lunch Ever in the back of his car. He hadn't spent much, but he hoped his effort might impress her.

She didn't flinch when he put an arm around her and leaned in to kiss her cheek. He took it as a good sign, and helped her into his car.

"It smells wonderful in here." She glanced at the backseat, which was full of goodies. "Are we having a picnic?"

He winked at her as he fastened his seat belt. "Clever girl, as always. I thought it would be more comfortable and it's such a nice day."

As if on cue, the sun came out from behind a bank of fluffy clouds. Sarah sat back and they made small talk as he drove through town. He'd already picked out a spot beneath the trees on the Campus Quad at the University. His ulterior motive was to evoke memories of the old days, when they were together and in love.

She helped him set up the blanket under a stately oak tree and unpack the bags of food. He poured the cider into small plastic wine cups, and held one up in a toast. "To memories, and the future, whatever it may hold."

She saluted with her cup, green eyes flashing anxiety for just a moment. Then she gave him a polite smile, before gazing out over the grass. He handed her a plate with cheese, bread and pate, and they ate in silence for a few minutes.

"This is delicious, Chris. You didn't have to go to such trouble."

"No trouble, Sweet. I had the time."

His old nickname for her slipped out, but she seemed not to notice. He couldn't help it, it felt so natural to be with her again. But time was a precious commodity, so he continued, "Tell me about your daughter. How old is she?"

"Sophie's five, going on twenty-five. I swear she stuns me with her questions sometimes."

"Smart, like her Mama, huh? Did your mom get to see her?" Her face fell, and he immediately regretted his question. "Sarah, I don't mean to pry, it's just...we are kinda beyond small talk. I want to know how you've been, what's happened."

Her glare told him he'd touched a nerve. "Oh, so you waltz back into town after all these years and expect me to jump back into your arms, and to tell you every little thing you missed?"

"It's not like that, but I'm here now, so yes...I do want to know. But I don't expect—"

She cut him off, rising to her knees on the blanket. "Let me tell you then, what happened after you left for California. I had to watch my mother suffer through a slow, agonizing death. Radiation treatments, chemotherapy, medicines that made her sick. She was so weak at the end, I had to do everything for her. Then I had to bury her. I had few friends or relatives to help me, and I was so messed up and lonely, I made the mistake of having a one night stand. The contraception failed and I ended up pregnant."

Chris felt his mouth open and close. He rose to his knees and touched her arm. "Sarah, I'm so sorry you went through all that. But you changed your phone number without telling me, and didn't answer my letters. I thought you had moved on, and didn't want to hear from me."

She shrugged and pulled away, but he leaned forward, putting his arms around her. Her body was tense, and he knew she was trying to hold back from crying. What must have been years' worth of frustration and bitterness were evident in the hard edge of her voice.

"The phone got shut off. We didn't have much money, and I just couldn't deal with explaining everything. I didn't want your pity. And I didn't want you to feel obligated to come back just because I was in trouble."

He looked into her eyes, which were wet from the tears that threatened to spill. Placing a hand to cup her cheek, he whispered, "I'm sorry I wasn't there for you."

Her jaw tightened under his palm but she didn't pull away. He looked into her eyes for a moment, seeing anguish there, but then a flicker of something else. He'd seen that look before, long ago. *Desire.* Did she want him the way he wanted her? Her lower lip trembled, and her head tilted back, just a bit. *If I kiss her now, will it upset her?*

Taking a chance, he moved forward and brushed her lips with his own, feeling the tender ache in his heart. It killed him that he'd hurt her, but he hadn't known. At the time, he'd trusted she would tell him when she needed his help. Now he knew she was much too strong-willed for that.

The kiss deepened, and they were in a tight embrace. Shivers, tingles and a warm buzz traveled across his skin. The electric chemistry they'd had once was reignited as his tongue met hers. She kissed him back, but her breath turned into a sob and she pulled away again to sit on the blanket with her back to him.

Sarah reached into her purse for a tissue to dry her eyes. She hated herself for breaking down like this, but her dam of pent-up feelings had burst uncontrollably. Finally facing Chris about what happened was something she'd dreamed of for years, but in her fantasy, she'd been way more in control of herself. "Just give me a minute, Chris. I never thought I'd get the chance to tell you how I feel."

His hand rested on her shoulder, causing the tingles to start again. His touch was wonderful and horrible all at the same time, because it evoked such a strong reaction in her. Their long-ago connection, both physical and mental, hadn't been imagined. It was real, but now it only complicated their situation.

"Take all the time you need, Sweet. I'm right here."

Damn him for being all caring and considerate now. It would be easier if he'd be the bad guy again.

It was true, he was here now, and seemed to care what had happened to her. She felt the ice around her heart start to melt, and the hurt begin to ease. "I know it wasn't your intention to hurt me, but I guess in my grief I had to blame someone. So I'm sorry, too."

His voice behind her was soft. "It's okay. I only wanted then what I want now, for you to be happy."

She smiled at that, turning back to face him. After a long, slow breath, she began to feel calm again. But her voice still shook with emotion, though she tried to control it. "And I wanted you to be happy, too, but I'm ashamed to admit I ended up resenting you for it."

"I understand, it all must have been hard for you. But…how are things going for you now?"

There was no mistaking the sincerity of his question. He really did care. "I'm okay now, most of the time. Things were tough for many years, but with Zac and Amanda's help, we got by. And soon, we'll be on our way to Sedona, and a new life. I've been offered a pretty good position there, so things will be okay for us."

He smiled, the skin at the edges of his dark blue eyes crinkling. *Age looks good on him. He seems calmer, wiser.*

"That's great. I'm about to make a change, too. Going back to New York, to work at one of my dad's companies."

He refilled her glass with cider, and she nibbled on some grapes. They were back to small talk, which was a relief, now that some of the emotion of the past was out of the way. Her lips still buzzed from their kiss, but she tried to ignore it. An image of both of them naked in bed came to her mind, but she

knew it was dangerous territory. Why subject her heart to being broken again? Especially this time, when she knew they
had no future?

When they finished eating, she glanced at her watch. "I
have to get back to work. But thank you for everything."

When they reached her office parking lot he walked her to
the door, his hand at the small of her back. She felt the urge
to move away but didn't. Torn between wanting him to leave
and needing him to stay, she said nothing. When they stopped
in front of the door, he also seemed reluctant to leave, holding
onto her hand. "I'd love to see you again, maybe tomorrow?
My plane doesn't leave until Sunday."

"I don't know, Chris. I need to pack, to spend time with
Sophie..."

The truth was, she wanted to spend the entire weekend in
bed with him, exploring each other in as many dimensions as
they could, but if they really did have that same connection,
it might be too hard to let go when the time came. Better off
to avoid it altogether.

He kissed her forehead, the heat of his lips making her
quiver. He pressed a piece of paper into her hand. "You think
about it. Here's the number to my room, if you need me."

She watched him drive away before entering the building.
An odd mixture of relief and longing settled over her. Would
she ever be free of Christian Levine, or was he in her blood,
and in her heart forever?

~*~

At four-thirty, Sarah left her office under skies that were
threatening rain. When she reached her Honda, she was
blocked in by a motorcycle, and the tall blond guy leaning
against her hood was none other than Wes Porter. "You're in
my way. But I guess you know that."

She unlocked her car, intending to ignore him. But he was at her side, helmet in hand. "Sarah, wait. I wanted to apologize for my horrible behavior yesterday. Funerals bring out the worst in me."

She leaned against the door, looking up at him. His expression was serious, so she relented. "Fine, apology accepted. Now I have to get home, so..."

He simply stood there, unmoving. "Thank you. I would hate to think you didn't like me. In fact, I really would like to make it up to you. I regret that we didn't see each other after our...well, tryst, way back when."

His reference to their one night stand made her wince, and she didn't know what to say. After an uncomfortable moment of silence, he asked, "I overheard you at the wake saying you have a daughter, right? I'd like to give you these."

He handed her two tickets to the carnival that was camped on the edge of town, which Sophie had been begging her to go to. They were for the next day, Saturday, the final day of the carnival. It was tempting to take him up on it, just to let her daughter have a little fun before they were uprooted. She took the tickets from his hand, putting aside her irritation at his apparent eavesdropping on her conversation with Chris. "Thanks, Wes. You didn't have to do anything."

He smiled, and just for a moment, she could bask in his good looks and forget his obnoxious side. Maybe he wasn't so bad, when he was sober.

"I'd be pleased to escort you and your daughter. Just to show you I can be a gentleman."

Her thoughts whirled. Once she left Colorado, she'd never have the opportunity to find out what kind of guy Wes really was. She'd rather have Sophie meet him under controlled circumstances, rather than when she was older and it was out of her hands how it happened. Maybe the man deserved a chance, maybe he didn't. But she would never know if she didn't spend some time with him, observing. "Actually, a day out might be nice. We can meet you there. Say, about eleven?"

As she drove home, she wondered if she would come to regret agreeing to a day with Wes. But she didn't have to decide anything just yet.

Why was it, as soon as she made plans to leave Fort Winston, it seemed the two most important men in her life were doing everything to keep her there?

6   The Hope

Saturday morning, Chris had a leisurely breakfast before heading up the winding road to Powder Keg Canyon. Despite their heart to heart talk, he still wasn't sure where he stood with Sarah, so he needed a place to think. The drive helped to clear his head, and soon he felt the urge to meditate, which he hadn't done in years. There was something about the beauty of the Rocky Mountains which reminded him maybe there was a greater power at work, and he desperately needed to tap into that.

He parked in an old campground, and was surprised he had recalled where the turn off was to find it. Not much had changed, and he easily found the trail leading up the mountain. Hiking in the higher elevations always made him hungry, so he brought a plastic bag with a few bottles of mineral water and some snacks. As he followed the old familiar trail, flashes of days gone by paraded through his mind. Some brought a smile, some made him sad. The overcast sky put him in a pensive mood, perfect for the soul-searching he'd put off for so long. When he finally reached the ledge he had visited so often before, he sat down to rest.

Though he was used to jogging for exercise, the thinner air made walking an effort. Calming his breathing, he searched in the bag. Wrapped in a towel was his special crystal, the one he'd found so long ago. It had been packed away, but he had discovered it in the back of his closet and brought it with him. He wasn't sure why. Maybe he was secretly hoping for a chance to use it again with Sarah.

If the thing even works anymore. This particular crystal had once seemed to amplify his power to astral-project his mind, inducing vivid out of body experiences. He'd had the power on his own since he was a child, but then it had only

happened in dreams. Strange dreams where he seemed to be
sleepwalking, but never physically left his bed. But his real
breakthrough came once he meditated with this crystal during
his college days in Fort Winston. Then his psychic abilities
expanded beyond anything he'd ever imagined, and it always
seemed to be sharper and clearer when he used the crystal.

He'd been so convinced the crystal was his ticket to prov-
ing his out of body experiences were real, he bet his entire
career on it. He'd impressed the faculty at the Noetic Science
Foundation with his purported abilities, only to find when he
got to California the damn thing no longer worked. He tried
several times, but it was no longer a special conduit for his
psychic powers. It was just a pretty, nine-pound rock. They
kept him on, anyway, but despite enjoying his work there he
always had a sense of falling short of his potential.

He glanced now at the rock wall to his right, noting the
bushes and trees overgrown in a tangle. He knew behind those
bushes was a secret cave, hidden from the world. It was filled
with artifacts and crystals, and the walls of the cave were decorated with strange symbols. When he'd found the cave years
ago he took the crystal as a memento, never realizing the role
it would play in his life. Even if the thing was useless now, it
had brought Sarah to him, and that he'd never regret.

Laying the crystal on the towel in front of him, he closed
his eyes. He focused on his breathing, letting go of the jumbled thoughts occupying his brain. A breeze ruffled his hair,
bringing the scent of fresh spring grass with it. The far-off cry
of a hawk faded away, and a feeling of calm spread through
him. As he felt himself go deeper, he wondered if he still had
the ability to move his mind beyond his physical body.

He thought he could sense the power of the crystal, could
still hear it singing to him. It might be his imagination, but
there was a low hum, barely audible, that thrummed through
his chest. He thought it might also be emanating from the
crystal cave; maybe it was one of those vortexes he'd read
about. He didn't believe or disbelieve, instead taking what he
experienced through his senses as proof. He concentrated,

waiting for the whoosh of sensation that always presaged his out of body adventures. But as the minutes ticked by there were no great revelations, no spiritual excursions, no psychic insights.

Only images of Sarah, reminding him of how alone he was.

Giving up, he flopped onto his back and looked up at the sky. It was a blank canvas, grey-white and empty, much like his soul.

When had he lost himself? It had been a long, slow slide. How did he go from having it all figured out to not even recognizing who he was, or where he wanted to be?

"I'm too young for a damned mid-life crisis."

He spoke aloud, the sound of his voice bringing him back to reality. So he'd gambled and lost. It wasn't the end of the world. He could lose the condo, his money, and his credit, but he still had some fight left in him. He had talent, he had skills, and would always find work, somehow. But what he could never replace was the feeling he had with Sarah, and he was not about to let her slip through his fingers again. She'd been angry at him, and he understood why, but there was passion in her kiss, and hope in her eyes.

He had no idea how, but he was going to win her back. He'd hate himself forever if he didn't at least try. He knew it might mean disappointing his father once again, and he had no clue what he'd do about his debts if the condo didn't sell soon. But if she would have him, he'd follow her to the ends of the earth this time. Everything else would have to be figured out later.

Wrapping the crystal back in the towel, he placed it in the bag. He ate his sandwich, his confidence returning. When he stood to walk back down the mountain, there was a spring in his step, and his heart was full of hope for the future once again.

~*~

Sarah was surprised at how excited Sophie was to go to the carnival. It made her realize how few things they did together, out of the house. She vowed to take her exploring more often when they got to Arizona. There would always be work and other obligations, but time with her daughter was limited and therefore precious.

The weather had turned cool and overcast, so they both wore denim jackets. Sophie had insisted on wearing her hair in a side pony tail, like she saw girls wearing in a video on the music channel. Her chosen outfit was a flower-print dress over leggings, and Sarah shook her head at the idea of her five-year-old worrying about the latest fashions.

"Today is just for fun, but you can't dress like that when you go to school," she admonished Sophie, while putting her own hair into a matching ponytail. She also wore leggings, with an oversized shirt cinched at her waist with a wide belt. Casual, and not the sort of outfit to give Wes any ideas. She hoped.

As they left the apartment, she took Sophie's hand. "Remember, I told you my friend, Mr. Wes, will be joining us at the carnival."

"Uh-huh."

"So be polite and remember to say thank you. He bought us the tickets."

"Okay, Mamma."

She could have said King Kong was meeting them and it wouldn't have mattered to Sophie, as long as she got to go to the carnival. Minutes later when they arrived at the parking lot, she saw Wes standing by the entrance. Her stomach knotted again, and she told herself it was just an experiment, nothing more. The purpose was to observe him and how he behaved, and more importantly, how he interacted with Sophie. Her daughter looked more like her, but had the same denim-blue eyes and blond curls, the same sturdy build as he did. Would he notice?

"Morning, pretty lady. Who have we here?" Wes crouched down to look at Sophie, and held out his hand. When she delicately touched his hand, he shook it once.

"Sophie, say hello," Sarah prompted. She did, in a small, shy voice.

Wes grinned, his eyes crinkling at the edges. Sarah noted how much he resembled Sophie for a fleeting second, and then it was gone. "Nice to meet you, Miss Sophie. Are you ready to see the carnival?" She nodded her head several times. He rose up, and offered his arm to Sarah. "Let's go then, ladies."

Over the next few hours, her opinion of Wes improved. He was polite, and wouldn't let her pay for anything. They rode on as many rides as Sophie could handle, they ate corn dogs and ice cream, they played games and he even won a stuffed Pink Panther for Sophie. He took control, guiding them around the place, suggesting what to do next. Sarah thought it was kind of nice to not have to make all the decisions for once.

Later, as she watched from the railing of a small corral, Sophie sat atop a cream-colored pony while Wes walked next to her. Several other parents or older siblings were alongside children riding the slow-moving ponies who were trudging in an endless circle while tethered to a central pole. The children were either squealing with joy or looked dazed; Sophie was neither, sitting regally, like a princess on her throne. Sarah took a photo with her camera while Sophie and Wes waved. Then her mind began to spin, the significance of the event known to no one but her. *Will this be the only photo of them together?*

Later, after they had made their way around the carnival twice, Sophie yawned. "I think she's had enough fun for one day," Sarah said, picking her daughter up. Sophie twisted, trying to get down.

"I wanna stay. I wanna ride the ponies again…" Her face grew pink with rage, and the overreaction told Sarah she was right. Sophie didn't often throw tantrums, but the stimulation of the carnival had wound her up. Tears spilled down the girl's cheeks, and she repeated her plea.

"Please, Mamma? Just one more ride?"

"No, baby, we have to get going."

She looked at Wes, but he was already walking over to the ticket booth. He returned a minute later with a ticket in his hand, and he waved it. "I just happen to have another ticket for the pony rides."

Sophie's tears stopped instantly and she clapped her hands. "Yay! Can I Mamma?"

Her own cheeks had grown warm, from irritation at Wes for overriding her without asking. How could she say no to Sophie now?

"All right. One more. Then we have to go home."

Wes held out his hand to lead Sophie to the corral, and Sarah nodded her permission. He winked, and she knew he probably meant well. He had no children, and didn't understand the importance of rules and boundaries. As she watched them walk away, hand in hand, she tried to reconcile the Wes she used to know with the man she saw now. Could people really change?

She still hadn't really forgiven him for the trick he played shortly after they met. At a gathering, he offered her a brownie that was spiked with drugs, and didn't disclose the fact. Eating it didn't hurt her, but it didn't endear him to her when she found out later what he'd done. And Zac had nearly beat the crap out of him for it.

But today, Wes Porter was all smiles and charm. He wasn't even smoking cigarettes anymore. Still, he had come on too strong at the wake, so what was the truth? Could she trust him?

After the pony ride, he swooped Sophie up and carried her, giggling, over to Sarah. She settled Sophie on her hip, and the girl's head fell onto her shoulder. "I guess we better get going. Thanks for everything, Wes. It's been fun."

He smiled at her, teeth so perfect he could have been in a dental office commercial. "My pleasure. I had fun, too. I love carnivals."

"I thought you'd be bored, after all of your adventures. You've travelled a bit, haven't you?"

His hand at the small of her back as they walked was strangely comforting. "Yes, I've been to Europe twice, Brazil once, even Japan."

"Wow. That's cool."

All things considered, the day was a success. Until his hand strayed lower than the small of her back. They were almost at her car, so she moved out of reach and set Sophie down, keeping hold of her hand.

"So, Sarah…Can we get together again? Maybe just you and me?"

His eyes were so hopeful, she almost believed his groping was an accident. Her opinion of him had improved, but she wasn't ready to spring anything on him just yet. But if she was ever going to tell him about Sophie, it had to be soon. The question was, how to do it? More importantly, what would he do? Would he try to stop her from leaving the state? There was so much to consider.

She opened the car and settled Sophie in the backseat before answering. Then she turned to him and touched his arm. "I'm leaving for Arizona in a few weeks, so I have no interest in dating, Wes. I'm sorry."

"Well, I can always come to Sedona for a visit. I love to travel, after all. Something tells me it'd be worth it just to see you."

His finger caressed her jaw line, ending at her lips. He licked his own lips, then he backed away, blowing her a kiss. "Let me know if you change your mind, I'd love to take you out for a farewell dinner."

She waved, and got in her car, more confused than ever about Wes Porter. Who was he, and did she really want to find out?

~*~

It was late afternoon when Chris found the address he'd been looking for. He'd forgotten Zac's last name, but when Sarah mentioned it, he'd recalled it long enough to look up the name in the phone book. As he pulled up to the ranch-style duplex, he saw Sarah's Honda in the driveway. It was a little creepy to track her down this way, but the ends justified the means.

He walked to her door, holding the single pink rose he'd bought, and a box of animal crackers for her daughter. His heart was beating a little faster as he imagined Sarah's face. In his mind's eye, it was a thrilled expression, but as he rang the doorbell he braced himself.

She opened the door, her hair swept up in a side ponytail. She looked even younger than she was, and her dimpled smile made him almost sweat with relief. Then her brow furrowed. "How did you know where I lived? I didn't tell you."

Busted. "I found Zac's name in the phone book. Sorry if it seems weird, but I really need to talk to you." She hesitated, then looked past him as Zac emerged from his door with a dog on a leash. The dog barked, more a welcome than a warning, and Chris walked down the steps to meet them.

"Hey, Zac, right? Been awhile, man." Chris extended a hand, and he shook it, switching the leash to his other hand. The dog sniffed Chris's legs, almost wrapping around him. Zac pulled the dog away with a jerk of the leash.

"Frodo, no. C'mon." He pulled the dog along, saying, "Good to see you," over his shoulder, but the man was clearly not interested.

Walking back to her door, he chuckled. "Seems he still doesn't like me. Or is he this way with all the guys you date?"

Sarah laughed. "The short answer is yes, but actually, you and I aren't dating."

"Ouch. Well, can I still come in? I promise to behave." He mentally crossed his fingers behind his back and handed her the rose and the cookies.

She looked over her shoulder, then held the door open. "Sophie's napping, but thanks for the cookies. She likes these. I'll put this in a vase." She took the rose to her kitchen, returning a moment later with it in a budvase. She set it on a table, then gestured for him to sit. "So, what was it you had to say?"

They were on her sofa, face to face. The room was semi-dark, the drapes drawn. Somewhere a clock ticked, mimicking the beat of his pulse. "Sarah, I've been thinking about what you said yesterday. I want you to know I wish things had gone differently between us. I never meant to hurt you, and I'm sorry for any pain I caused."

She looked down at her hands. "I know. I'm sorry for my part, too. I shouldn't have blamed you. But it's all in the past, and you can move on now, knowing it's all okay."

There was a note of finality in her tone, and he felt the rise of panic. "But I don't want to move on. I want to be with you." It wasn't what he'd intended to say, but he meant it. He'd laid his heart on the line, and now it was up to her. He reached out to touch her hand, but she pulled it away.

"You can't do this to me now. It's not fair."

"I'm not trying to make you stay here, or go anywhere you don't want to go. I'm just telling you how I feel."

She covered her face with her hands for a moment. When she raised her eyes to look at him, he saw so much emotion. Pain, regret, sadness…and a glint of something else. *Love?*

But when she spoke her voice was calm, no trace of the emotions he saw in her eyes. "Okay, so now what do we do? Will you move to Arizona with me? I have to be honest, I can't imagine living in New York City. For us to be together, one of us has to change our lives, and I wouldn't want you to give up your life to be with me, and then regret it later. Besides, I come with extra baggage now. Sophie and I are a package deal."

Her words hit him like a hammer. Did she think he was so shallow, that he wouldn't consider her child?

"I know that. I don't have much experience with kids, but she's yours, a part of you. I don't know how or where we could work things out, I only know I want to try. Sarah, I don't want to lose you again. If that means following you to Arizona, then I'll find a way to make that work."

He held his breath. To his surprise, she moved closer, and took his hands in hers. "We both have a ton of unresolved emotions over this, Chris. Maybe that's all this is. Although, I do still feel some of that special bond we had, don't you?"

He gulped and nodded. The heat from her hands was soothing, and her pulse was in rhythm with his. "I do. That's why I'm here."

"But we're not kids anymore. We have responsibilities. Just like before, though, our lives are being pulled in opposite directions. I'm flattered you would be willing to give up your plans to be with me. But it'll never work, no matter how much we want it to."

A tear slipped out and she pulled her hand from his to wipe it away. In his heart, he knew it was risky, foolish even, to follow her and turn his own life upside down. Was it just unresolved feelings driving his desire for her? Or were they meant to be together?

Before he could respond, she sniffed back another tear and said, "A wise man once told me, that it didn't matter how much time we had together physically, because we would always be connected because of our psychic bond. He said our souls are entwined, and always will be."

He knew she was speaking words he'd told her long ago, when he was young and idealistic. The sentiment of it might still be true, but the words were no longer a comfort to him. Instead, he felt his heart ripping in two.

"Yeah…Words of wisdom." He gripped her hand tight, needing to get through to her. "Sarah, I don't know what the future holds for either of us. But can't we make the most of the time we do have, right now? Please say you'll have dinner with me tonight. Then if we still decide to go our separate ways, at least we'll part on good terms this time." It wasn't the outcome he wanted. But it was going to take time to convince her he was sincere and to figure out how to resolve his own situation.

She smiled, a sadness still lingering in her eyes. "Yes. I'd like that. Let's make it a night to remember."

She leaned in and he kissed her, a slow, gentle kiss, full of promise.

7 The Truth

Sarah had Sophie fed, cleaned, and in her pajamas by six o'clock. She carried her next door, so Amanda and Zac could watch her while she had dinner with Chris. Amanda met them with a glass of tea for Sarah. "Come sit for a few minutes. Zac's teaching Frodo some new tricks in the backyard."

Sophie perked up and ran to the back door. On slippered feet she went down the steps of the back porch to join Zac, who was putting a spin on his Frisbee toss. Frodo jumped in the air to catch it, missing the pink disc and slinging slobber in the air. Sophie giggled and shouted, "Do it again!"

Sarah sat on the wooden bench at the edge of the back porch and Amanda maneuvered in beside her. "So where is he taking you?"

"We decided on Ernesto's. We used to go there back in the day, one of our regular haunts. I haven't been there in years, forgot about it."

"Well, it is way on the other side of town. El Gato Blanco is closer, if you like Mexican food. But what I really want to know is…will you be home by morning?"

Sarah elbowed her. "Mandy, quit it. I told you, this isn't like that. It would be a really bad idea to sleep with him."

"Mmmm hmm…so why are you blushing?"

Her cheeks did feel hot. It was difficult enough to keep a rein on her desire for Chris without Amanda pushing her over the edge. "My life is already complicated, thank you. But I do need your advice on something else."

"Sure, anything."

Zac was still entertaining Sophie as they ran back and forth around the yard, but Sarah kept her voice low. "You know I never told Sophie anything about her father, and she's started asking questions about him. I guess the baby coming has made her more curious about things."

Amanda's hand went to her belly, a subconscious gesture. "That's natural. What are you going to tell her?"

"That's just it. I'm not sure whether she's better off not knowing anything. I know so little about him myself. But if she finds out anything when she's older, I might not be there to help her through it."

"I can see that. But whether you tell her now or she finds out later, she may want to contact him at some point. Do you think she'll even have any luck in trying to find him? You said you never could."

It wasn't exactly the truth, but she hadn't lied, either. After she'd discovered she was pregnant, she told Zac and Amanda she knew who the father was, but he was just some guy she met at a club. Which was all true. The only thing she left out was the fact they knew him as well. When she had tried to find Wes, he was out of the country, and his family said he'd be gone for months. So she kept her secret and moved on, determined to take care of her child alone.

"I don't know. Maybe it's better to leave him in the past. I have no idea how he would react, or what he might do if he was here now."

That part was true, except for the 'if'. Wes was here, in her life again, but what did she really know about him? There was the Wes she'd known since school, a pretty-boy, a player, and a smug jerk most of the time. But their time together yesterday made her think maybe he'd matured. Technically, he had a right to know he'd fathered a child, but was he a threat to the welfare of that child? She had no idea how he might react to the news. Amanda was silent, leaving her to her thoughts, so she continued thinking out loud.

"Sophie is the most important thing in my life, and I want to protect her. I've always felt that I was doing so by keeping her father's identity a secret. It was just a one-night stand, and I wasn't able to find him afterwards, so I just kept going on with my life."

Amanda held her hand, squeezing it. "I know it's been tough, and you've been a great mom. I can't tell you what you should do. But I'll support you in any way I can, whatever decision you make. And I'm sure Zac will, too."

Sarah squeezed Amanda's hand in return, and rose to leave. She knew Zac was even less fond of Wes than he was Chris, but there was no reason to discuss it. "Thanks, hon. I don't know what I'm going to do without you."

Amanda stood to walk her out. "There's always the telephone."

She said goodbye to Sophie and Zac, and went home to wait for Chris to arrive. As she sat on the front step of her porch, it struck her she was being presented with an opportunity to wrap up loose ends before she left town. Both men were important to her, for different reasons. She decided to make amends by being honest with them, and with herself.

~*~

On the way to the restaurant, Chris was glad to find Sarah in a chatty mood. They talked easily, with none of the awkwardness he feared might be there after baring their true feelings for each other. He was also encouraged by the short make-out session they'd had at her house earlier, kissing on her sofa, being quiet like they were two teenagers trying to avoid being discovered. But they were discovered, when Sophie woke from her nap and stood staring from the hallway.

Sarah had pulled away, leaping for the box of animal crackers he'd brought. The distraction worked, and soon Sophie was dunking them in a cup of milk, and smiling at him. She had a front tooth missing, and a milk moustache. She couldn't have been more adorable.

"She's a mini-version of you. What's not to love?" he said later, as they laughed about the incident.

Sarah huffed. "Oh, God, I hope not. She does have a mind of her own, though."

Ernesto's looked in need of a makeover, but the scent of grilled meat and exotic spices brought back memories as soon as they entered the place. They were seated in a booth, and ordered flavored margaritas, just as they'd always done.

"I can't believe they still have apple margaritas. I haven't had one in years," Sarah said, taking a sip, and licking the cinnamon-sugar on the rim of the glass. "Mmmm. Still so good."

They chatted for a few minutes, then Sarah's tone turned serious. "I think Sophie might have some psychic abilities. I haven't told anyone, but you might have some insight on this."

She described the strange dreams her daughter had, which sounded eerily similar to his own experiences with astral projection. The girl's dreams included the sensation of leaving her body, and going out of her house to walk around at night. Although Sophie never actually left her bed, she was accurate enough in her descriptions of things she saw or heard while supposedly traveling to give Sarah reason to be concerned.

Chris agreed it was a concern, but tried to put her at ease. "Wow. That's amazing, for her age. I didn't have true out of body episodes until I was older, sometime before I met you. But I had similar dreams when I was young, and my family thought I was making it up. But to me it was so vivid, so real. Eventually it stopped, but I never forgot any of it. In fact, that's what made me curious to learn about what my mind could do. Which also led me to study psychology. So, this indicates she has some creative power. It's a good thing."

"I thought so, too. But I worry she'll actually wander out of the house sometime. It's just odd, you know, after what happened with us? I can't imagine how she has the same abilities as you."

The waiter appeared with their food, and for a few minutes they dove in, making pleasurable sounds of appreciation. When they slowed down, he ordered her another margarita. She protested at first, then gave in with a sheepish look. "They are really good. Don't know when I'll be back here."

He picked up their conversation again, eager to discuss something they could both relate to. "Maybe Sophie will find her own soulmate someday, who can astral project with her, keep her safe." His target had been hit, if the look in Sarah's eyes were an indication. They had deepened to an olive green, and there was a light he'd thought he'd never see again. Then she looked down at her plate.

"Chris…"

He took her hand over the table, caressing her fingers with his thumb. "All I'm saying is, it's a good thing for her. If you're worried, lock all the doors with deadbolts. But don't try to hold back her interest in it. Who knows what she can do with it? It's similar to what brought us together."

"Maybe. I knew you'd understand."

"From what I hear, there are plenty of psychics and shamans and enlightened people in Sedona. She'll fit right in."

Later they were driving across town and the conversation lagged. The turnoff that led back to her house was coming up, but he didn't want the evening to end so soon. He was trying to come up with a suggestion when something she said earlier triggered the solution. "Damn, Sarah, it's too bad we didn't have a camera. Remember the first time we went to Ernesto's? I still have a photo of us, drinking those apple margaritas. It would have been cool to have an updated one."

"Yes, that would've been awesome. I have a few old photos from those days, too. I think they're already packed up, though."

He paused at the traffic light. "Well, Celia gave me some old photos, and you're in some of them. They're back at my room, if you'd like to see them. If you're not too tired, I mean."

He waited while she looked at her watch, then glanced out the window. "I don't know…I really should get home."

Traffic ahead of him started to move as the light changed. "My hotel's not far, you won't be that late. This might be the last time we have together, you know." He didn't use the guilt tactic often, but he couldn't let her go without trying something to get her to stay. Maybe she felt the same, or maybe it was the margaritas, but she relented.

"Okay, but just for a few minutes."

~*~

Sarah knew she'd made a mistake as soon as she entered his hotel room. Being alone like this was only going to make it harder to resist him. Now the spicy food had made her thirsty and the two margaritas made her woozy, so when Chris offered her a glass of water, she gulped it down.

"Are you okay?" he asked, leading her to the bed.

She sat down, yawning. "I'm sorry. I haven't been drinking much lately. Guess it got to me."

"No problem, Sweet." He handed her an envelope he'd pulled from his suitcase. "Here, look at these."

In the envelope were photos, most of Dr. Engle, but some of her and Chris. "Look at your hair," she told him, laughing.

"My barber loves me now. Back then, he'd have gone broke waiting for a visit from me."

She had loved his long brown locks back then, but the layered cut he now wore suited him. She realized he had matured, and seemed more serious, not only in his appearance but his demeanor. His passionate nature seemed a bit more subdued. She hesitated, then asked him for the truth. "Chris, are you happy? I mean, about moving to New York to work for your dad?"

Her question must have caught him off guard. He stared at her with a frown, before coming to sit next to her on the bed. "To be honest, no. At first, I wanted so much to impress you with my accomplishments, but spending time with you has reminded me you're the only one I could really be myself with. You know some of my deepest secrets, Sarah. So it makes no sense to pretend everything is going great, when my life has slowly turned to crap."

It wasn't what she'd expected. She'd sensed an underlying tension in him, but was so wrapped up in her own feelings and problems, she hadn't considered what might be the cause. "I'm sorry to hear that. I figured of all the people I knew, you were the one who'd be successful. What happened?"

He lay back on the bed with a huff. "Everything. Nothing. Too much, and not enough."

She leaned on her side to look at him. "Now you're just being dramatic."

"Maybe. It may have been poor choices, bad luck, or a combination of both, but taking the job in New York will solve most of my immediate problems. I've had some financial issues recently, so I 'm selling my condo and have to move anyway."

They were inches apart. She could feel the heat emanating from his leg next to hers. Her brain was pleading with her to move away, but the heat was drawing her closer. He rolled onto his side and with one arm pulled her to him.

"I'm glad you told me the truth," she whispered. "Now I don't feel like I'm the only one who's had it rough."

"You've been through much worse than I have. You're amazing."

She knew he meant it, and something finally clicked into place in her heart. She'd forgiven him for the past, knowing that if they had stayed together, she wouldn't have Sophie. Maybe life had gone the way it was supposed to, for both of them. "Thanks. I've been on my own for a long time."

She didn't back away when he leaned in to kiss her. It was a slow, sensual kiss, and she felt the passion he was holding back, the underlying tension of his desire. That same tension coiled under her skin, almost aching for release. It would be so easy to let go and give over to pleasure. But she knew that pleasure came with a price.

His tongue sought hers, deepening the kiss. His hand on her hip, kneading and caressing, made her own hands itch to feel his muscles. She ran one palm over his back, straying lower until she felt skin where his shirt ended. He broke the kiss to press his lips against her neck, moving downward. Behind her closed eyes, colors started swirling, and she felt herself slipping into a dream-like state. Making love had always been more than a physical act between them, and she could sense the blending of their minds as keenly as she felt the heat of his firm body against hers.

He murmured against her ear, "Baby, I've missed you so much. I want to make it up to you, to love you so good and so hard you'll never forget me."

His words took her breath away. It was what she'd longed to hear for years. But alarm bells were ringing in her head, and she said what she never thought she'd say. "Chris, please. Stop."

He froze, pulling back just far enough to look in her eyes. In his sapphire-blue depths, she saw disbelief. There was a note of pain in his voice. "Why?"

She pulled away and sat up, smoothing her hair. "I'm sorry. I'm just afraid..." She paused, recalling her earlier promise to herself to be honest. "I'm afraid if we make love, losing you will hurt all over again. Maybe even worse this time."

He kneeled in front of her and took her hands in his. "I get that. But I'm taking that same risk, maybe even more. I told you I'll give up everything to be with you this time. I don't even know how I'll take care of my own shit, or even what kind of work I'd do in the middle of the freakin' desert. But I want to be with you, and that's all that matters."

He kissed the back of her hands, and she felt the tears welling up again. *Can't we just talk without tears?*

"I know you really mean what you say. But is it possible you're speaking from guilt? I know I was kinda mean to you at first, but I had years of resentment and anger built up. Not just about you, but about my mom's illness, about having an accidental pregnancy, being a single mom, giving up my career...everything. My life hasn't turned out the way I'd hoped, either. I don't want us to be together simply because we think it will solve all of our problems, because it won't."

He stood, pulling her up with him. Then he leaned forward, touching his forehead to hers. "Sarah, I don't know how to convince you that I've thought all this through. I know it seems sudden, but it's actually the culmination of years of feelings. Everything came together for me the minute I saw you at the wake. When that guy started pawing you, I had to step in. I want to be the one to help you, to protect you, to make sure you and Sophie have everything you need."

The armor she'd erected around her heart softened a bit. To her surprise, his pledge to protect her caused her desire for him to flare, making her skin heat again. It was her primal need for a strong mate responding, but she ignored it. Right now her intellect was still in control. "Awww...I loved that you did that, I was impressed." She laughed softly, and so did he, still holding her close. "But this has happened so fast, and I have so much going on in my life right now. I need some more time."

He released her, and she went to the restroom to freshen up. A few minutes later they left, and he drove her home. They talked about people they once knew, what San Francisco was like, and how Sophie learned to walk. They didn't talk about their feelings for one another or what the future might hold.

At her door, she promised to call his room in the morning. He kissed her again, and she wondered if it would be their last.

8 The Plan

Sunday morning, Sarah was having coffee and looked out her kitchen window to see Zac in the yard. He was preparing to mow the grass but stood watching as a black BMW pulled up to the curb. When Wes Porter unfolded his tall frame from the car, she nearly dropped her mug.

What the hell is he doing here? She was beginning to feel claustrophobic, like there was no place she wouldn't run into old lovers. Who was going to turn up in Sedona? Or would the desert be her salvation, where she could finally find peace from her past?

She was dressed in sweats and wore no makeup, but she didn't care. Zac was shaking his head, no doubt telling Wes to get lost. She considered staying hidden, then decided to find out what the hell was really going on.

"There she is. Thanks anyway, man."

Wes's voice was polite, but there was an undertone of annoyance. Zac still protested. "Sarah, is this guy bothering you? 'Cause I'll—"

She put up a hand as she walked toward them. "No, it's okay. We met up at the wake."

Zac stopped, but watched them with wary eyes. She gave him a look she hoped conveyed that she was in control of the situation, then turned to Wes. "What are you doing here?"

"Good morning to you, too." There was a touch of sarcasm in his voice and it was beginning to irritate her. "I wanted to invite you and Sophie to brunch."

"Well, she's already had her breakfast." Thinking she still hadn't decided what, if anything, to tell him about Sophie, she offered a compromise. "Would you like some coffee, though?"

His face brightened, and he glanced over at Zac, who was back at the mower. "Sure, I'd love some."

As they walked to her door, she heard the sound of the mower revving up, and saw Zac give the mower a shove. She needed to explain a few things to her best friend, but now was not the time.

Sophie was still in her pajamas watching cartoons. Wes greeted her and she waved, smiling her gap-toothed smile. It was a small blessing that Sophie looked more like her, though she did resemble him in subtle ways. The color of her eyes, the dimple in her chin. If the resemblance had been more obvious, she might have been forced to explain.

One step at a time, McKenn.

She handed Wes a steaming mug of coffee, and they went to the back porch, where Sarah had spoken with Amanda the night before. Both sides of the duplex shared the porch and yard, and Frodo came running to greet them. Wes patted the dog on his head, then turned to Sarah. "I'm so glad we could talk. I just wanted to see you again."

"I'm flattered, but I still don't understand why you wanted to see me."

She really didn't. He looked every bit the preppie today, with his pastel blue Izod shirt, khaki pants and leather loafers. Back in college, he'd had long-ish hair, and dressed more casually, probably to fit in. Now he looked like a rich man's son, and she knew he probably had girls falling over themselves to date him.

"How can you say that? I've had a crush on you since...I can't even remember when. I told you that when we got together that night in Denver."

The gleam in his eyes told her he hadn't forgotten their tryst in the back of his car. A shudder ran through her, but she forced a smile. "Well, I was not myself at the time. My mother had just died and I was kind of messed up."

He sipped at his coffee, probably wondering how to respond. Then he looked at her, and she saw some compassion in his eyes. "I don't think you told me about that, so I hope it's not too late to say I'm sorry. I'd had a bit to drink that night, too. But I can't say I regret it. Being with you, I mean."

She'd always figured he'd forgotten her. What was a one-night stand to a guy like him? He could have any girl he wanted, and had a reputation of serial dating, rarely having a girlfriend. Then it occurred to her that was all she really knew about him. The current subject was making her uncomfortable so she asked, "So do you work for your father now?"

"Yeah, he's a dentist. He runs more than one practice, though. I started dental school a while back, but it wasn't my thing. Now I do advertising and promotion for the chain."

"Wow. Guess you're doing pretty well then."

"You could say that. But I get restless. That's why I travel whenever I can, but I also work to feed my hobbies."

"Which are?"

"You saw my motorcycle, right? I love anything where I can get out and ride. I have a four-wheeler, two Jet Skis, and a speedboat. Started taking flying lessons once, too. Maybe I can take you and Sophie on the lake sometime."

She smiled, instead of reminding him again she was leaving soon. It was a moot point. So he was not a horrible person, but still seemed immature and scattered. Not the type of guy to willingly take on the responsibilities of a child, if she read him right. The only way to find out for sure was to tell him her secret, but now was not the time, with Sophie close by. She wanted to deal with one dramatic moment at a time. But if she was going to talk to him, it had to be soon.

"So, Wes…is the offer still good to go to dinner with you, alone? I'd like for us to end on a good note before I leave town." As soon as the words left her lips, the feral glow she'd seen before returned to his eyes. Before he could respond, she added, "I mean, just as friends. Please don't get the wrong idea."

His grin was one of embarrassment. "Was it that obvious? I guess I can't help it, I still have high hopes."

She chuckled, in spite of her misgivings. "So, tonight? If I can get Zac and his wife to watch Sophie."

"Yes, I know just the place. There's a great steakhouse downtown. Near the Cellar bar. Maybe we can go there for drinks afterward, I heard they sometimes have live music."

She knew about the steakhouse, one of those old-time places with overstuffed leather booths, dim lighting and dark red tablecloths. The food was superb and the wait staff excellent, so she agreed. It seemed like a quiet place to have a serious discussion. He would return for her at seven, and she hoped the night would end with them on good terms.

~*~

After a restless night, Chris spent the morning on the phone. Sarah said she needed more time, so like the lovesick fool that he was, he'd arranged it. He'd figured out which credit cards he still had room left on, and changed his travel plans. He'd called the realtor, who'd told him she'd shown his condo a few times, but still had no bites. A newer development just down the street was attracting most of the buyers, but she assured him she still had interest. As usual, timing wasn't going to be on his side.

He'd saved the worst for last, calling his father. "I just need a few more days, maybe a week at the most."

Joachim sounded patient, but his tone was laced with a warning. "It doesn't help your credibility, son. After the credit concerns, delaying your starting date is not going to look good. I've told them you're a professional. Don't let me down."

There was an excellent possibility he was going to let his father down. If he had to go to Arizona, and forget New York altogether, his father's trust in him was going to be shattered. It was already fragile after he'd changed his course of study in college, before he'd told anyone. It was only after he'd secured his move to San Francisco to work for the Foundation that he'd revealed his change of plans to his family. It wasn't what his father had wanted for his eldest son, who he assumed would take over the family business, and it had taken years for their relationship to repair.

So now Chris was about to let the man down for the second time in his life. "I'll do my best, Pop. I'll keep you posted."

If it turned out there was no hope for him and Sarah after all, then he'd go to New York and give it his best shot. He'd throw himself back into his work, as he'd done before. Even if he hated it, and it drained the joy from his soul, he'd do it, because that was what was expected of him. He'd just have to learn to live without her, forever this time. But he wasn't giving up until he was certain he'd tried everything in his power to make it work. He'd given up too easily before, and it had cost him.

He'd just gotten dressed and was about to get a late breakfast, when Sarah called his room. Her voice was friendly, but there was a distracted edge to it. After he told her he wasn't leaving as planned, she hesitated.

"So…what about your new job?"

"I talked to my dad. It's cool, they'll wait for me. Are you busy today? Can I see you?" There was silence on the line, and his heart sank. He was twisting the cord in his fingers, biting his tongue so he wouldn't seem too eager.

"I really have to pack today, I'm so behind. You can come over and help, I guess. If you don't mind."

"Sure, I don't mind at all. How 'bout I pick up a pizza on the way?" His stomach was gurgling and he worked better when he wasn't starving.

"Sounds good. Sophie just likes plain cheese."

Less than an hour later, he was at her door with pizza in hand. She had made a salad and the three of them ate lunch in the kitchen. He'd also picked up some brownies from a local bakery, and Sophie ended up with a chocolate frosting moustache.

Sarah winked at him. "Her moustache reminds me of yours, back in school."

He winked back. "Ah, I miss those days of not having to shave."

"You look good, either way."

She smiled, and his hope raised, just a bit. "So, what's on the agenda?"

She had him pulling things from the higher shelves so she could wrap them in newspaper. Some items she had him take to the back bedroom, where she was storing things she wasn't going to take with her. He set down a full box in the corner, pausing to look at an antique desk. It was an old roll-top, with rows of small drawers along the upper edge, larger ones below. Papers, notebooks, and envelopes covered every surface. A stack of journalism periodicals stood a foot high on the floor next to the desk. It seemed she'd never totally let go of her dream of being a journalist, and traveling the world. He felt a pang of sadness at the sight of Sarah's forgotten dreams the desk represented.

When he returned to the living room, he asked her about it. "You're not going to take that awesome old desk? It's pretty cool."

She frowned. "Wish I could. I can't really take any furniture. No idea how big our apartment will be. My friend Nadine has lined up some places for us to check out when we get there. But we might have to stay with her or in a motel temporarily."

The thought of her and Sophie living in a motel, even for a short while, bothered him. But he didn't want to start that discussion with Sophie there. He returned to the job of moving boxes from one place to another, and a few hours later, they stopped for a break.

Sophie had fallen asleep on the couch within minutes, and Sarah led him outside to the front porch. Sitting on the steps, they sipped sparkling water. Sarah glanced at the plastic watch on her wrist more than once, and his stomach clenched. "Do you have plans this evening, Sweet?"

Her lowered eyes told him she did even before she admitted it. "Yes, I'm having dinner with someone. Not leaving until seven, though."

"A date?" He'd kept his voice level. No need to act like the jealous suitor, even though that's exactly what he was.

"No, just a friend. We have some...stuff to discuss."

The tone of her voice said it was serious. He wanted so much to know everything about her life. It took every ounce of control not to ask her for more, so he just said, "Oh. Well, I was hoping to have dinner with you tonight, but...how about lunch again tomorrow? Your choice, this time."

She sighed, and gave him strange look. He'd promised to give her time, which was one luxury he couldn't afford. But pushing her wasn't going to help his case, either.

"Call me at work tomorrow around ten. I should know how my day's going by then. I may not be able to break away for lunch."

It wasn't much, but he took it. "Okay. Should we finish up those last boxes, then?"

It felt good to help out. He was tired of waiting around, and every minute he spent with her was a blessing. The looming threat of her moving far away from him was still there, but he was trying to make the most of each moment until he ran out of time.

~*~

Amanda had agreed to watch Sophie again, showing up at Sarah's door just as they were ready to leave. She was beginning to feel as though maybe she was taking advantage of her friends' good nature, with all these unexpected plans, but she had no choice.

"Sorry. I was on my way, just getting Sophie's coloring books so she'll stay out of your hair." Everything was a mess, with boxes and stacks of newspaper all over. "God, I hate moving. Can't find anything now."

"It's okay. I'll help her find them. Zac wants to talk to you."

Sarah paused to look at her friend, whose voice had sounded serious. "What is it?"

Amanda knelt down to help Sophie, who was digging through a box of toys. "He just has stuff on his mind, I guess. He wouldn't tell me. But let me know later, please?"

She winked, so Sarah figured it couldn't be too bad. "Will do. Not sure what time I'll be home, but I doubt it will be too late."

She grabbed her purse and walked next door. She was casually dressed, not for a date but for dinner with a friend, in her long skirt and a buttoned-up ruffled blouse. The last thing she wanted was to encourage Wes's wandering eyes; she needed him to take her seriously tonight.

Zac let her in, and they sat at the kitchen table. "Want a beer?"

"No thanks. Have to leave soon, so...what's up?"

He hesitated, his cocoa dark eyes looking around the room. Then he ran a hand through his bushy hair, assessing her. "Sarah, I'm worried about you. No other way to say it."

"Well, thanks. I appreciate it, but you really don't need to be. Sophie and I will be fine in Sedona."

"That's not what I'm talking about, and you know it. First, Chris Levine shows up out of the blue, then Wes Porter, of all people. You've been hanging out with both of them. What's really going on?"

She stared at him, her lips tight. If it had been anyone else, except maybe Amanda, she'd have told him to mind his own damn business. But they'd always been close, and had helped each other through the worst of times. It made sense he would be concerned, and she loved him all the more because of it.

"Nothing, Zac. I'm just wrapping up some loose ends, I guess. I ran into both of them at Dr. Engle's wake, and they wanted to catch up. They both know I'm leaving soon, so it's nothing for you to worry about."

His long fingers strayed to the whiskers on his chin, the goatee neatly trimmed. In his hippie days, when she had first met him, he'd resembled a cave man with his wild hair and beard. Now he looked the part of a family man, albeit still a little scruffy. His expression was one of doubt. "Why do I have the feeling you aren't telling me everything?"

Because I'm not. "You better get used to it, Big Brother, 'cause pretty soon I'll be in the next state. Then you really won't know what I'm doing or who I'm seeing, will you?"

She'd meant it as a playful taunt, but his face reddened. "Laugh at me if you want, but I know what those guys are like. Chris left you when you needed him most, and Wes…he's just an ass. He'll use you then toss you aside. Neither one of them is worth of a minute of your time, Sarah."

He got up and shoved his chair, almost knocking it over. His display of anger surprised her, but she couldn't blame him. He only saw what he saw. He didn't know the whole story and telling him the truth about Wes right now wouldn't help the situation. Still, his words caused the fragile hold she had on her emotions to crumble. Though she had made peace with what had happened in the past with Chris, and with Wes, the hurt hadn't totally subsided.

She crossed to where he stood in the kitchen, looking out of the window. She touched his back, and he didn't move away. "Zac, listen. I hear what you're saying. And you're not totally wrong. But you'll have to trust me this time. I have to take care of things my way. I know what I'm doing."

I hope.

He turned, moving away from her. Opening the fridge, he pulled out a can of beer. After he opened it he took a long sip, then looked at her. "I hope so. I trust *you*, but I don't trust *them.* That's all I'm gonna say."

She walked over and hugged him, and he hugged her back. She placed a hand on his cheek and said, "Thank you." Outside a horn honked and she left him standing in the kitchen, alone.

9   The Truce

Cordon's Steak House was just as she remembered it. Her office had a luncheon there years before, and it still smelled of leather and spice. The wait staff wore crisp white shirts and thin black ties, ushering them to a booth lit by soft golden candles. There was already a silver basket on the table, filled with fresh baked bread which smelled heavenly.

Wes ordered the wine, showing off his knowledge of French vineyards. The waiter was patient, standing by as Wes recounted his travels in Europe, explaining why he thought European wines were superior to domestic. Sarah only smiled, recalling how the same guy had preferred beer and pot when she first met him in college. It seemed he'd made peace with 'the establishment' after all, becoming one of them.

They discussed the menu while waiting for their drinks. Sarah's stomach was fluttery, knowing the discussion she was about to have, so nothing sounded appealing. When the waiter came back, Wes ordered a chateaubriand for the two of them.

"It's a house specialty. My family comes here whenever they're in town. My Dad knows the owner, and my cousin's the manager here."

Wes hadn't been exaggerating, and every few minutes, someone stopped by the table to say hello. A well-endowed cocktail waitress came by, blushing and winking at Wes, then the tall, blonde hostess smiled seductively as she passed, followed by a group of guests.

"You're quite popular here, Wes. Especially with the ladies."

He grinned, and took a sip of wine. "I try to be friendly with everyone."

His modesty wasn't fooling her, but she let him get away with it. She listened as he continued to talk, telling tales of his travels. He was obviously trying to impress her. She wanted to bring the subject to a more personal level, but each time she was about to speak, someone brought food or stopped to talk to Wes.

"Maybe I should have taken you somewhere quieter. Like a bowling alley," he quipped, making her laugh.

"I always thought this place was pretty sedate. But not tonight, I guess."

Later, she declined dessert, but accepted another glass of wine. The knot of tension in her neck had left, and her stomach had settled. "The chateaubriand was phenomenal, Wes."

"I'll tell the chef."

The voice had come not from him, but from a woman standing at their table. She was dressed in a black pantsuit with padded shoulders, and there was a silky floral print scarf at her neck. Her chestnut hair was teased high on her head, and her face held a professional smile.

Wes nodded, indicating the woman. "Sarah, may I introduce my cousin, Marlene James. Manager of this fine establishment."

"Nice to meet you," Sarah said, extending her hand across the table. Marlene shook it, then slid into the booth next to her.

"Likewise. Now let me warn you about this guy."

For the next few minutes, Marlene and Wes sparred, trying to outdo each other with good-natured insults. Sarah glanced at her watch, aware of the time passing by. Her plans were not unfolding as she'd hoped. She finished her wine, feeling like a third wheel when she'd hoped to have Wes's undivided attention. Finally, Marlene stood up. "Sorry I crashed your date. I'd better get back on the floor. It was nice to meet you, Sarah."

When Marlene left, the waiter brought the check. Wes took care of it and stood, offering her his arm. "C'mon, let's go somewhere more intimate. We can have a drink at the Cellar. An Irish coffee sounds good right now."

By instinct, she placed her hand on his arm. "Yes, it does. Maybe there, we can talk."

He leaned down and whispered, "My ears are all yours."

There was no mistaking the suggestive tone of his voice. She pulled away, pretending to search for something in her purse. Maybe it was best to avoid touching him at all, as he seemed bent on turning this into a more intimate evening than she had planned.

~*~

Chris showed up at Sarah's house, knowing she wasn't home. She was out for the evening with a friend, and he didn't want to speculate too long on who that might be. He walked toward the ranch-style duplex, carrying a six-pack of beer in one hand and a box of gourmet chocolates in the other. It wasn't Sarah he'd come to see, but her friends, Zac and Amanda.

Time was running out, and he needed reinforcements. Plus, if he was able to convince Sarah she truly was the love of his life and they were meant to be together, Zac and Amanda were part of the package. Even if they relocated to Arizona, he knew Sarah and Sophie would keep in touch with their dearest friends, so it was important he get to know them, and for them to like him. Zac had already made his disdain clear, so the beer was a peace offering of sorts.

He rapped on their door and waited. When Zac opened the door, surprise registered on his face. Then he glanced over toward Sarah's door, saying, "She's not here, dude. She's out for the evening."

The door began to close and Chris held up the beer. "No, this is for you. I know Sarah's out. I wanted to talk to you, and your wife. If that's okay."

Zac just stood there, looking at him through the screen. Amanda appeared behind him, peering over his shoulder. Chris held up the candy, and said, "A peace offering. I'm afraid we haven't really met properly, and you guys might have the wrong impression of me. So I wanted to make amends."

Husband and wife exchanged a glance, and Zac opened the door to let Chris pass. In the kitchen, he placed the beer on the table, explaining, "I wasn't sure what brand you liked, so I brought one I like, hoping you will, too." He handed the candy to Amanda, who smiled at him. Sophie was at her elbow, dressed in pajamas and holding a stuffed Pink Panther doll.

"Well, we like chocolate, don't we Sophie? Thank you, Chris." She let Sophie pick one from the box, and took one for herself. After settling Sophie on the sofa in front of the television, she returned to the table. Zac had opened one of the beers and handed one to Chris, placing the rest in his refrigerator. Then they both sat down as though they were about to have a business meeting, looking at Chris expectantly.

Now or never. You have to at least try.

"I don't know what you know about me, but I wanted to tell you that Sarah thinks the world of both of you. For that reason, I respect you and I'm grateful she had you to help her out all these years. Friends like that are hard to come by."

Zac's expression was still skeptical. "Sarah's like a sister to me, and I'd never let anyone hurt her."

His dark eyes held a warning, and Chris knew winning him over was going to take more than a six-pack. He was prepared to go the distance, so he answered, "I totally get that. I never meant to hurt her, either. What happened years ago, why we broke up, was a mistake. Bad timing and poor judgement. But we were young and were both handling things beyond our control. That's why I couldn't leave this time without making sure Sarah and I were on good terms."

Amanda said nothing, but her face had softened. Her fingers were fiddling with the edge of the placemat as she looked from one man to the other. Zac was sipping his beer, then he pointed a finger at Chris. "That doesn't change the fact you left her. She was all alone in Denver, caring for her mom. She gave up everything. We went down to visit her every chance we could, and she was just a mess. I'm sure you had your reasons, but the effect on Sarah was devastating."

"All true, Zac. I don't deny it. But did she tell you that even after we broke up, I tried to call her and wrote to her several times? But the phone was disconnected and I never got a response to any of my letters."

He looked at his wife, then back at Chris. "No. She didn't want to talk about you at all back then. So I assumed it ended badly."

"It ended, officially, on what I thought were good terms. I was upset about it, I didn't want to break it off, but she told me she no longer wanted to do the long distance thing. I knew she was going through all that with her mom, so I gave her some space. But it's not like we had a huge fight or anything."

The wariness had left Zac's face, so he continued despite the turmoil in his stomach over recalling how he and Sarah had parted long ago. "But let me tell you, guys—it hurt me, too, when she cut me off like that with no explanation. Maybe I should have dropped everything and came after her, but I eventually just gave up and moved on with my life. I never stopped thinking of her, of us. That's why I'm here now, why I couldn't just walk away after I saw her at the wake."

"You still love her." It was Amanda's voice, matter-of-fact, but filled with reverence. He wasn't afraid to admit it this time, not to anyone.

"Yes, I do, and I'm going to do whatever it takes to make her happy. The only thing that'll stop me is if she tells me to leave her alone. That's why I need your help."

10   The Secret

The wine had loosened her up, but Sarah's stomach still fluttered when she thought about telling Wes her secret. Now that he had reappeared in her life, she knew she'd drive herself crazy with guilt for not telling him, and would forever be wondering how he'd react to the news he was Sophie's father. The only way to find out for sure what would happen was to go through with it. She was still afraid he'd try to control her in some way once he knew, but she was the one who had the final say when it came to her daughter.

As he parked the car in the lot of the Cellar bar, she recalled the many times she'd come to hang out while Zac tended bar years earlier. They hadn't been there much in recent years, so the chance of running into someone she knew in the bar was slim. But Wes seemed to know people wherever he went, so the bar might not be the best place to talk. As he reached for the door handle, she touched his arm. "Wes, let's sit here in the car a minute. There's something I need to tell you."

His face had the look a man gets when a woman says she wants to talk—a mixture of dread and boredom. "Sure. What is it?"

Her mouth had gone dry, but she swallowed the lump in her throat and got to the point. "That night we got together in your car? Well...that was the night I got pregnant."

In the semi-darkness of the car, she saw his blue eyes go wide. For the first time, it seemed he was speechless, his mouth open but saying nothing. Then he ran a hand through his hair. "Are you sure? I mean…what happened?"

She had to believe he was in shock, because he could not be that dim. "I had a baby. My daughter, Sophie. You're her father."

He looked out the window, staring at the rows of cars. He held a finger to his lip, then made a sound of disbelief. "I'll be a son of bitch."

Heat rose in her cheeks. She didn't know why she was getting angry with him. What had she expected? "Is that all you can say?"

"Damn, Sarah, I had no idea...I don't know what to say, or think. Are you sure she's really mine? I mean..." He floundered, no doubt realizing the implication of his words.

Still, it irked her that he doubted her, after days of agonizing over telling him. "I wasn't having sex with anyone else at the time, so yeah. I'm sure."

He just sat there, shaking his head. "Wow." She didn't say anything else, giving him a moment to absorb the news. Then he added, "We used a rubber, didn't we? I know I was buzzed, but I'm usually careful."

She couldn't keep the emotion from her voice. This conversation was years overdue, and it wasn't any easier than she'd imagined. "I guess it broke. Something didn't feel right when we were, uh...done. Later, when I found out I was pregnant, I tried to contact you but you were in Europe or somewhere. I don't recall."

He had a faraway look, as though trying to remember that night long ago. "So I actually have a daughter...I'm sorry, I guess I'm just in shock." Unbuckling his seat belt, he opened the door. "Damn, girl. I don't know about you, but I need a drink and a moment to process this."

She got out, grateful for the cool night air. She stood, breathing deep. Her nerves were jangled, and she felt a little dazed herself. She decided to let him settle into the idea tonight, but tomorrow they would have much to discuss. As they neared the door to the bar, she touched his arm. "Please don't say anything to anyone else until we've had time to discuss things, okay? I've never told anyone else who Sophie's father was."

"Sure. No problem."

For once, his face was inscrutable, and she wasn't sure what he was thinking. She felt some relief from finally telling him, but she hoped she wouldn't come to regret it.

~*~

After an hour of chatting around the kitchen table, Zac had suggested they go shoot some pool at the Cellar Bar. Their honest conversation had cleared the air, and they'd ended up laughing about the old days at Fort Winston University. It turned out they knew some of the same people, and that led to poring through the old Fort Winston University yearbooks. Soon Amanda had put Sophie to bed and was yawning herself, so the guys decided to go out and continue their reminiscing.

Zac had stopped short of agreeing to help him win Sarah back, but said he wouldn't interfere. "The girl's got a mind of her own. But I guess you already know that."

They were perched on barstools, waiting for one of the pool tables to open up. Chris tipped his beer bottle in salute. "Yes, I did notice that about her. She can be a bit stubborn, can't she?"

Zac laughed. "Well, if you are the guy for her, she'll know it. It's not for me to say. But I'm sorry I misjudged you."

"How could you have known? There's always more going on than meets the eye, especially when it comes to dealing with women, eh?"

"You're not married yet, so you have no idea. Trust me."

Chris was about to respond with a joke, when he turned to see Sarah walk into the bar, with a tall blond guy right behind her. The same asshole who'd tried to maul her at the wake. His entire body tensed and he eased off the bar stool, standing rigid.

Zac turned in the direction Chris was staring. "Oh, crap."

"Who is that guy?"

"Wes Porter. Asshole extraordinaire."

"So why's she with him? I got the impression she didn't like him."

"I thought so, too. But he's been coming around since she saw him at the wake."

Zac's revelation made no sense whatsoever. Why would Sarah be on a date with the same guy he had to protect her from? Before he could think it through, she'd noticed them and was walking over, but she didn't look pleased to see either one of them. He had a feeling his luck had just gone from bad to worse.

~*~

As soon as they entered the bar, Sarah saw Chris and Zac hanging out together like they were bosom buddies. She had no idea how that had happened, but she was going to find out. They saw her approach and slid off their barstools, murmuring to each other.

"What are you guys doing here?" She was aware of Wes behind her, and looked from Zac to Chris, but neither man was looking at her. If they had been canines, not humans, fangs would be bared and snarling would be audible. Instead, both men stood next to their stools with rigid posture and narrowed eyes on her companion.

Zac spoke first, glancing at her. "Nice to see you, too, McKenn. Though I'm surprised at your choice of company tonight."

Wes moved closer behind her; she could feel the heat emanating from his body. *Oh, good Lord. They're starting a pissing contest already.* She moved a bit to the side to avoid being too close to any one of them.

"The lady has good taste. She's enjoyed her night out with a true gentleman so much, she didn't want it to end. So we came here."

Wes's voice was smug as ever, and he put an arm around her shoulders in a possessive move. She turned away, pretending once again to look in her purse for her lipstick. Without looking up, she said, "Actually we came here to talk."

When she did look up, the expression on Chris's face made her stomach drop. His dark blue eyes had gone almost indigo, and his face and neck were flushed. A muscle worked in his jaw, as though he was about to let loose. Instead, he took a long sip of his beer and leaned back against the bar, looking Wes over as if for the first time. "Hmmph. My first impression of you, at the wake, was that you're anything but a gentleman."

The smirk on Wes's face turned into a frown, and his fists clenched. *This is when they'd start sniffing each other...*she couldn't help but picture a dog fight shaping up, so she tried to intervene. "Guys, listen. We're just here to talk about something, so back off. Go back to being best buddies, have another beer. Later I want to hear how you two made up."

She smiled and raised her brows, hoping to diffuse the situation. They ignored her, staring at each other stone faced. Then Zac took a sip of his beer, and settled back on his barstool. His mocking tone was unmistakable. "Yeah, Porter. Since when have you become a gentleman? That's never been your reputation. I hear you're more of a love 'em and leave 'em type."

Zac had no way of knowing of the conversation she and Wes had just had in the car, but his accusation couldn't have come at a worse time. She watched as Wes crossed his arms over his chest, and took a step closer to his accuser. "Ya know what, dude? You think you know everything because you've been friends with Sarah? Trust me, she doesn't tell you *everything*."

This was heading in a nasty direction fast. "Guys, this is pointless-"

She was cut off by Zac, who'd jumped from his stool to poke Wes in the chest with a finger. "And you think *you* know her? Give me a fuckin' break."

Wes shoved his hand away. "I know her a lot better than you think, asshole."

Chris had moved between the two, and though he was a few inches shorter than Wes, his stance was menacing. "I know her better than both of you, so shut the fuck up."

Zac now turned on Chris, shoving him in the shoulder. "You're the reason she wants to leave Fort Winston. Too many bad memories."

Chris's face was inches from Zac's. "Maybe it's you she's running from. She doesn't need a big brother, she needs a man."

Wes laughed out loud, and both men pounced, shoving him into a nearby table. Empty glasses shattered on the ground as he grabbed the table to break his fall.

"Stop it! All of you." She did the shoving this time, pushing Chris who bumped into Zac, moving them away from Wes. He regained his feet, and she shoved him, too, until she had all three of them in a row, staring at her with expressions of surprise.

Patrons in the bar were also staring, but she didn't care. A burly man, probably the bar's bouncer, stood nearby, but Sarah waved him away. Then she crooked her finger to indicate she wanted the three to listen to what she had to say, and they moved closer. "None of you really know me, what's in my heart, so stop arguing about it. I've been trying to talk to Wes all night alone, and the reason for it is no one's business. So just leave us alone for a while, okay?"

Chris and Zac nodded, moving back to their barstools. She looked at Wes, and motioned for him to follow her. A booth at the back of the room was empty, and as she made her way toward it, she heard Wes's voice. "That's right, boys, I won. Neither of you will ever know her like I do. You better get used to it."

She stopped, unable to suppress an eye roll. This was getting old. When she turned back, Zac and Chris had both blocked the aisle, effectively stopping Wes in his tracks.

"What's that supposed to mean? You think you have some claim on her?" Chris's voice held a warning, and though she was secretly pleased he was coming to her defense again, she wanted to avoid another brawl.

"More than you'll ever have, so go back to wherever it is you crawled from."

Wes wasn't backing down, even though Zac was growling out his own warning. "If you hurt her, Porter, so help me God—"

She had almost reached them when Wes pushed both men out of his way. They pushed back, though, and this time the bouncer and another burly guy joined in, breaking them apart. She stumbled to avoid one of the bouncers, dropping her purse on the floor.

It was then she heard the words "father of her child" coming from Wes's lips, and she froze. So did Chris and Zac, each with a bouncer holding onto their arms.

"What did you say?" It was Zac, who looked from Wes to her, his eyes wild.

Wes straightened up, his smug smile returning. "I said, I'm the father of her child. Sophie's mine."

Bastard. He's actually gloating.

There was no other word for it. He glanced at her with a sheepish look, and shrugged. She was so pissed she thought it might take both bouncers to keep her from beating the crap out of Wes, and punching the other two for good measure.

Chris looked at her with such a pained expression, she had to look away. Zac stared at her, disbelief evident on his face. She nodded, and he closed his eyes, shaking his head. She stood there, holding her breath. No one spoke, they just looked at her, then looked at each other. Then Zac and Chris both blurted out the same words, "Are you sure?"

She picked up her purse and left the bar.

~*~

Chris's legs had turned to water but somehow he made it out the door. He found Sarah standing near one of the bouncers, who had followed her outside. He was talking into a hand held radio and ordering someone to call for a taxi. As Chris approached, the bouncer gave him a warning look.

"Sarah, wait."

She'd moved away when she saw him, going to stand near the edge of the building. "Just go. I don't want to talk to anyone right now."

Zac and Wes had followed him, both standing near the door, watching. They had the good sense not to bombard her, at least. Chris nodded toward them and turned back to Sarah, who wouldn't even look at him. "Sarah, I didn't know why you were with that guy. I thought he was trying to take advantage of you. I can't help but be protective, but I was out of line. I'm sorry."

She didn't look at him, her eyes were fixed on the road. She blinked a few times, and he thought she might be on the verge of tears. It must have been an emotional night for her, with her big secret revealed like that. He didn't know how he felt about her news. He only wanted her to not be angry with him. There would be time to figure out his feelings about the whole mess later.

When she finally spoke, her voice was thick with emotion. "Give me some credit. I may have made some mistakes in my life, and I'm sure I'll make some more. But no one else knows what's best for me and my daughter, but me."

The taxi appeared, and she climbed in. Chris leaned in the open window and handed the driver a ten. "Get her home safe, please." Then he looked at Sarah. "Call me tomorrow, okay?"

She nodded and looked out the window. He stood there on the sidewalk until the taxi was out of sight. Wes and Zac still stood near the door with somber faces. When he reached them, he said to Wes, "Well, I guess you do know her pretty well. Congratulations."

~*~

Sarah was glad she made it home before Zac. Amanda met her at the door, wearing pajamas, her red hair a tousled mess.

"Did I wake you? I'm sorry. It's barely eleven."

"It's okay. I never sleep for long now, anyway." She rubbed her protruding belly, and turned to the kitchen. "Want some tea? I've got an herbal blend that helps me to sleep."

Sarah let out a sigh. "Yes. That sounds wonderful. I need to tell you something, too." Amanda would find out soon enough, so she may as well be the one to break the news. When they were seated at the table with mugs of hot tea to sip on, she felt calm enough to laugh a little. "I had to break up a dogfight just now, involving your husband."

Amanda's ruddy eyebrows shot up. "Oh? Do tell."

She explained about the argument, and how Zac and Chris had thought they were defending her honor. Then she said the words she'd nearly told her friend three hundred times before. She'd always chickened out, but it was too late for that now. "Well, earlier I had finally told Wes that he is Sophie's father. But in the argument, he blurted it out, even though I asked him not to tell anyone. But man, you should have seen their faces."

Amanda's face registered surprise, but she smiled and sipped her tea. "You never mentioned Wes specifically, but now I understand why. He was never Zac's favorite person, to put it mildly. But is he really that bad?"

"No, I've come to learn he's not a horrible person. But he's also not ideal father material. And his behavior tonight proved that point."

"It must have been hard, keeping it a secret all these years."

"It was. Right after it happened—our one-night stand—I just wanted to forget him. I'd used him, and he'd used me. I thought that was the end of it, until Sophie came along. But I really do feel better now that I got it out. I only hope I can deal with the aftermath."

She'd have to tell Sophie soon. It might only confuse the girl, but in time they would deal with it. Though she was still angry as a hornet, she'd have to talk to Wes again, too. His first reaction, his intimation that there was a possibility that Sophie wasn't his, had hurt. Then Zac and Chris had echoed the same question. She knew it was a shock the way it had been revealed, but the humiliation and fear she'd spent years overcoming had risen up to consume her again, due to their disbelief. So she'd walked out.

As if reading her mind, Amanda asked, "So what did Wes say, when you told him?"

"He was stunned, as they all were."

"Has he even seen Sophie?"

"Yes, he spent the day with us at the carnival yesterday. She seemed to like him."

"Well, if you're still planning to leave for Arizona, he can't do much, can he? Like stop you from leaving?"

"I hope not, because I'm still planning on it. I don't know what he wants, since we didn't get a chance to talk about it. I'll have to deal with it tomorrow." She finished her tea, and put the cup in the sink. "Thanks for listening. Now, I better get my sweetie home and into her own bed."

She carried her sleeping daughter from Amanda's guest bedroom to her own place next door. As she placed her on the bed, Sophie opened her eyes long enough to sleepily murmur. "Mamma, that was a pretty yellow car."

"What yellow car, honey?"

"The one you came home in."

The taxi. Sophie had been sound asleep the whole time, since she arrived and during her conversation with Amanda. The guest bedroom was at the back of the house, so there was no way her daughter could have seen the taxi. Unless she had "dreamed" it. "Yes, it was pretty. Were you outside tonight?"

She snuggled into her pillow, blue eyes half-closed. "Only for a minute. I was looking for you."

Kissing her daughter's cheek, she whispered, "Well I'm right here now, so you can go to sleep."

And please stay there.

As much as it worried her, Sophie's nighttime "wandering" was also fascinating. She wondered if it was anything like her own experiences with Chris, some form of astral travelling. Mind out of body stuff. But concerns for her daughter's safety overrode her curiosity, and she decided it was better to wait until she was a bit older to discuss it.

Sarah pulled the door almost shut, leaving it ajar in case Sophie needed her. She was eager for her own bed and the bliss of sleep, ready to put the events of the day behind her.

11   The Agreement

Chris left the bar once Sarah had gone. He still felt like beating the crap out of that Wes guy, for his lack of respect for Sarah. He told them later he hadn't found out until tonight that Sarah's daughter was his. But that didn't give him the right to be an asshole about it. She was clearly upset when Wes revealed it, and he and Zac questioning her didn't help. He never meant to imply she didn't know for sure who the father was; it was just that Wes Porter seemed like the last guy she'd have chosen to be with.

One thing he knew for sure—Sarah McKenn was never the type of girl who'd sleep around. She wasn't a prude, by any means, and had a wild side when it came to sex. But a one-night stand with a guy she didn't even like? It seemed so out of character for the woman he thought he knew. Had she changed that much?

Possible scenarios of what may have happened to cause Sarah to get together with Wes paraded through his mind, keeping him from sleep. Kicking off his sheets for the third time, he punched his pillow in frustration. He knew he had no business trying to figure out her past. He loved her, and that was all that mattered. What happened to either of them in the years they were apart was just stuff they'd have to deal with, if they ended up together. Now he realized why she was so reluctant to get involved, even though it seemed she really wanted to be with him. She was thinking of her daughter first, and though he didn't like the idea, Wes was now a part of Sarah's baggage, too.

What will happen now? What if Wes makes demands? This was a distraction he couldn't afford. He had a few more days, at best, to win Sarah back, to convince her they belonged together. Her hesitation made more sense now but was still an obstacle.

He had to walk a fine line between pursuit and allowing her space. In the end, the decision was ultimately hers. All he could do was pledge his love and she would accept him as he was, or walk away. He had to get to her heart somehow, to break through the distractions of the drama with Wes, and show her what she meant to him. Words were simply not enough.

In the darkness of his room, he walked the few steps from his bed to his suitcase in the corner. He unwrapped the crystal from the towel protecting it, and held it up to the moonlight streaming in through the curtains. A subtle vibration tickled his fingers, running up his arms. He placed it on the mattress, sitting cross-legged nearby. Breathing deep, he closed his eyes, found his center and began to slip into a relaxed state. The tension he'd felt earlier slid away, replaced by a sense of calm. Blurred images, fuzzy blobs of color, coalesced in his mind's eye, turning into shapes. The shapes became clearer, and though his eyes were closed, he could "see" his room. Soon he began to feel the sensation of floating outside of his body once more. It was subtle at first, just a light buzz across his skin, but the sensation grew as he slipped deeper into a relaxed, semi-conscious state.

I can still do it. Awesome.

He felt an old familiar rush and he was rising, up and out of his body. He saw himself below, cross-legged on the bed in front of the crystal. His "vision" had a fuzzy distortion to it, as though he was looking through a filter. He experimented, turning and moving around the room. After a few seconds, he was able to control his being's movement with ease, just like before.

Why couldn't I do this for so long? Is it Fort Winston? Or being near Sarah?

Thinking about what was happening, and trying to make sense of it messed with his concentration, so he let go of his concerns for the moment. There would time to contemplate later, but right now there was something else he had to do.

Passing through the wall of the room, his disconnected-self floated outside. He could feel, but not like having skin. It was more of a vibrational change, intensifying the moment he passed through the wall, and smoothing out as he resumed floating in the open air. He could see where he was going, drifting along as one might float in deep water, being carried but still able to change direction at will. He found as he gained control he could accelerate his speed, and he did so, heading in the direction of Sarah's house. He wondered as he drew closer if what he was about to do would be considered spying. He only wanted to check on her, and doing so in the flesh while she was still angry was a bad idea.

It was well past midnight and the streets below were quiet, save the occasional barking dog. It amazed him he was able to see and hear so much; it had been years since he'd astral-projected his mind like this. Something about Sarah and the strong emotions she caused in him must have been a trigger. His astral "body" began to vibrate strongly as he hovered over her house. He'd never felt anything like it before, it was a strange tingling, some sort of warning, though he felt no sense of danger. No one else could see him or sense him, after all, and even if they did, he could will himself back to his room at a moment's notice.

The light of the full moon illuminated the yard, and he hovered over the walkway near the front door. It seemed ludicrous to worry about how to enter the house when he could just as easily pass through a door as he could through a wall or a window, but he didn't want to alert her to his presence. He was counting on her being asleep, but if she wasn't, he'd have to get away without being noticed. She'd seen him do this before, so the possibility was real if she was awake.

He decided to go through the window, as it was thinnest. The vibrational buzzing was less noticeable than when he went through the wall, and he continued into the darkened living room. It seemed she and Sophie were asleep, and he floated down the hall to Sarah's room. She lay on her side, clutching her pillow, with her gold-tinted brown locks pulled into a ponytail by a soft cloth Scrunchie. He floated a moment, watching her breathing, and fought a strong urge to lay down next to her and enfold her in his arms.

"You came to visit."

The voice behind him was soft and childish, and another vibration, one of shock, rippled through him. He turned to see Sophie in her pajamas, looking up at him. But it wasn't her, really, because she was floating above the floor—just like him.

"You can see me?" he asked, knowing it sounded stupid, but unable to process the enormity of the situation. The girl nodded, and rose up a few inches from the floor, as though to get a better look at him. He could see her, too, but he could also see through her. She was visible, but not really a part of her surroundings. She seemed curious, but unafraid. Still, he felt compelled to comfort her. "I just came to say goodnight. To make sure you and your mom were all right."

Sophie nodded, and moved back a bit, towards her room. "Okay. Momma's sleeping."

He looked back at Sarah, who snorted as she rolled over. Could she sense their presence? When her breathing settled, he looked back at Sophie, who was still hovering, bathed in a soft, blue glow. "Yes. I'm glad you're both okay. But don't tell her I came, it might worry her. Our secret, okay?"

"Okay. But will you come back again?"

They were talking, but not audibly. He thought what he thought and she heard him. She said her words, but her lips never moved. It was some sort of crazy telepathy, similar to what he had experienced with Sarah years before. Was there something in her blood, in her DNA, that connected her to him in this way? Whatever the cause, it was phenomenal, and was beginning to freak him out. "Yes, Sophie. I'll be around."

She began to float backwards, the vison of her fading. "Good. 'Cause Mamma loves you."

She disappeared before his eyes, and he turned to look at Sarah, who was still sleeping, blissfully unaware of the exchange that had just taken place in her bedroom.

She loves me. If Sophie thinks so, it must be true.

As he floated back to the hallway, he passed Sophie's door. He peeked in to see her snuggled down in her blankets, sleeping as soundly as her mother. Another shiver passed over him, as he made sense of what just happened. Would she remember their encounter? What would Sarah think if she found out?

In moments he was back through the window, raising up over the trees and in the direction of his hotel. When he emerged from his astral body, and was back to his flesh and blood self, he lay back on the bed, the words of a little girl echoing in his head.

She loves you.

~*~

Sarah made it to her office with minutes to spare. It was her last week at work, so she probably wouldn't get in trouble if she was late, but being on time was her habit. Anytime she had been late, it was usually due to Sophie not waking up on time or dragging her feet getting ready.

Like this morning. She slept all night, yet she was still so tired.

Every time her daughter had one of her "dream-walking" episodes, it seemed to wear her out, and last night must have been a doozy. She'd barely kept her head up at breakfast, mumbling something about talking to a man.

But that couldn't be right. All the doors and windows had been locked; she'd double-checked them as Chris had advised. Unless she'd gone outside in her dream-state, and talked to someone. Either way, it was becoming a real concern.

She shook out her umbrella as she entered the foyer, and removed her raincoat. She needed coffee, so she made her way to the breakroom before going to her desk. Martina was already there, munching on a donut. Her grin was even perkier than normal. "Good morning. You must have had quite a weekend, Ms. McKenn."

She almost spilled her coffee as she poured the fragrant brew into her cup. "It was okay. Why?"

"Because you have three messages already. From guys."

"Everybody wants to see me now that I'm leaving," she mumbled, more to herself than in answer.

"That'd be my luck, too," Martina said, handing her a donut. "The messages are on your desk. Happy Monday."

One of the messages was from Chris, with the number to his hotel. *He must be worried, after I stormed out like that.* She didn't blame him for being protective. He had no way of knowing why she'd been with Wes. She liked the idea of Chris fighting another guy for her more than she should—some sort of inborn reaction to chivalry. Recalling how close they'd come to making love when she was in his room made her shiver with desire, and she sipped her coffee, palming the mug in both hands. If she didn't have Sophie to worry about, she might have given in and slept with him. They probably would have spent the entire weekend in bed. It was still a temptation. Though she was the one who had put a halt to it, the idea of never seeing him again and not knowing how it might have been between them caused her longing for him to increase.

The second message was from Wes, just a phone number. It was a local exchange, so he was likely staying with friends. It was doubtful he'd simply disappear after the bomb she dropped last night. She felt a little guilty now, not giving him a chance. But he had pissed her off, blurting out her secret in a crowded bar just so he could win a stupid argument.

The third message was from a property management firm in Sedona she'd called inquiring about apartments for rent. She promptly returned the call, and a young-sounding guy answered the phone. His name was Blake Haswell, and he told her he had some information for her.

"Right now, Sedona is booming," he informed her. "It's hard to find good apartments for rent, but there are a few new projects being built. One is almost completed, and it's close to where you said you'll be working. There's also a new mall opening up close by, so it's convenient to shopping. Plus there's a New Age learning center that holds classes, like yoga and hypnosis, right across the street. It's very popular, they even have a small health foods market."

Wheels started turning in her head. This was really happening, and a brand-new apartment sounded awesome. "When will the new complex be open for rental? And how much per month?"

They discussed the features of place, and they had some models that would fit her budget. She'd have to find temporary housing until she went through the approval process, but they could be in a new apartment within a few weeks. Nadine had said she had a large house where they could stay, and she'd have to take her up on it. She thanked him and was ready to hang up, when she asked, "Does the Learning Center also need instructors? I know someone who teaches meditation techniques."

The words came out of her mouth before she realized it meant she was actually thinking of him moving to Sedona. *Well, it can't hurt to find out some information.*

"I'm sure they must. I can give you their number."

Mr. Haswell was pleasant and helpful, answering all of her questions. She promised to meet with him as soon as she arrived in town, and hung up the phone feeling more hopeful for the future than she had in years.

Next, she called Chris, but there was no answer in his room. She left a message with the front desk, and then dialed the number Wes had left. Another man answered the phone and soon Wes was on the line.

"Hey, Sarah. I'm so sorry about last night. I didn't mean for things to get so out of hand."

"Well, you weren't the only one to blame for that. I'm not happy with how you handled it, but I know it must've been a shock."

"Yeah, you might say that." An undertone of sarcasm was evident, but he changed the subject. "So can we get together?

I'd like to talk about this soon. I have to go back to my parent's place in Denver tomorrow at the latest, 'cause it's my sister's birthday."

Everything was happening so fast. It was as if the moment she decided to change her life, it became a runaway train that was about to derail any second. She had so much to do to prepare for the move, and now all of this. Still, putting off talking about their situation would not make it any easier. "Can you meet me for lunch? Trinket's diner downtown is within walking distance of my office. Hopefully the weather will clear by noon."

He agreed, and she spent the next few hours trying to focus on work, but the knot in her stomach had other ideas. Eventually Chris called her back, and he wasn't happy to hear she had lunch plans.

"You're seeing him, aren't you?"

"We have a lot to talk about." The hesitation in his voice told her he was trying to be polite, but she knew it must be hard for him. When he spoke again, she also heard resignation in his tone.

"Well, just let me know when you have some time. The last thing I want to do is pressure you, Sweet. I just want to spend time with you before you leave my life forever."

If he was shooting for making her feel guilty, he succeeded. The truth was, when they parted, it just might be forever, since they'd be once again be separated by distance.

Time. It was the one thing she had precious little of at the moment. She hung up, determined to somehow make things right with everyone involved.

~*~

The rain had stopped and her walk to Trinket's diner helped to clear her head. The aroma of grilled cheese greeted her as she reached the door, and her stomach grumbled. Eating properly had been low on her list of to do's lately.

Wes was at a booth, and he stood to greet her, kissing her cheek. The intimate gesture felt awkward to her, but after all, he was the father of her child. Though it was true, it still felt weird to think of him that way.

They talked about the weather, her work, and his sister's birthday dinner at his parents' house the next evening. The waitress brought their food, a cheeseburger for him, grilled cheese and tomato soup for her. After he took a few bites, he set the burger down and looked her in the eye. "Sarah, why the hell didn't you tell me when you first found out? We used protection, so I figured we were safe."

"I know we did. But as I mentioned last night, protection doesn't always work."

"I guess not. But you still should have contacted me at some point. It's been, what? Six years?"

"Roughly. Sophie will be six in September, on the ninth." She looked away, still finding it hard to talk about that time of her life. But he was here, and he had a right to know. "I wanted to tell you, at first. I found your parent's number in the phone book and called, but they told me you were gone for several months. Backpacking across Europe or something. So I just went on with my life."

His denim-blue eyes, so much like Sophie's, had a far-away look. *The same look she gets sometimes, when she's lost in thought. Now I'll always think of him when I see that.*

"Yeah, that was a crazy summer…in fact, I goofed off most of that year. Then Dad lowered the boom and I had to go to work."

"How sad for you." She couldn't keep the contempt out of her voice, recalling how tough it was to make ends meet in those lean years after Sophie was born. With Zac and Amanda's help, she made it through, but it was never easy.

"Nah. I needed a kick in the pants. I do like my job, now. At first, I resented it, family business and all that. My parents wanted us all to go into the dental field. I'm the only one who rejected it. But I like sales and marketing, I'm good at it."

She didn't doubt that. With his preppie good looks and family connections, he would do well for himself. Which didn't necessarily mean he'd make a good father for Sophie. "I'm glad. But you can't just show up now and expect to be accepted. Sophie and I have been on our own forever, and we're leaving soon. I don't think it's a good idea to upset her right now. Maybe someday things can be different, but for right now…"

The hang-dog look in his eyes threw her off. She'd always pictured him as the careless playboy, and maybe some of that was a device to assuage her own guilt for not including him. But the fact remained, they were leaving town next week.

He looked down at his plate, and dragged a French fry through a puddle of ketchup. He popped it in his mouth, and looked at her with hopeful eyes. "Tell ya what. Come with me to Denver tomorrow night and meet my family. You and Sophie can stay in our guest room overnight if you like. My sister has three kids and my brother has two, all under the age of twelve. It'll be fun. Then you can judge for yourself if you want to be part of the Porter family or not."

The idea was daunting, unaccustomed as she was to large families. But what better way to see what Wes and his family were really like? Her curiosity overcame her trepidation, and she considered it. "I have to work the next day, so we wouldn't be able to stay overnight. And please don't tell your family about this, until we agree. It's a lot to absorb for now, you know?"

He agreed to drive her and Sophie home after the event. They finished their meal, and the rest of their conversation was pleasant. He asked questions about Sophie's birth, how she grew, what her personality was like. Sarah found herself feeling more comfortable, but she still couldn't picture what the future might be like with him in it.

12   The Longing

Since Sarah was busy, Chris spent most of Monday in the local library, reading up on Sedona, Arizona. There wasn't much current information, but he did get a feel for the location and learned the history of the town. It was an up-and coming tourist area, but still small, population-wise. Phoenix, the closest large city, was a few hours away.

It sounded like an interesting place, but he had no idea where he'd find work if he moved there. The whole mystical-vortex-New-Age-philosophy reputation of Sedona did interest him, since he'd made a career of studying and testing the power of the human mind. Or, he'd tried to. He hadn't done much metaphysical research since his early days at the Noetics Foundation. It would be ironic if he ended up somehow re-connecting with that kind of work.

Right now, what he did for work wasn't as important as being with Sarah. He'd follow her to the ass-end of the earth, if that was where she wanted to go. He was still young, strong, and willing to do whatever he had to. Material things, like his condo, were just that—things. What was most important to him now was being healthy and having someone to love, who loved you back.

When he returned to his room around four, the front desk had a message for him. It was Sarah's work number, so he called, hoping she'd decided to have dinner with him. Hearing her voice on the line still excited him, and he hoped it would always be that way.

"I still have some more packing to do, but you can come over if you want. I should be home by five."

"Great. How 'bout I bring Chinese food this time?"

"That'll work. Sophie likes the noodles."

"You got it."

He hung up the phone, wondering if Sophie would remember their encounter the night before. If it even happened. After he slept for several hours, it all seemed like a strange dream. But the crystal lay on the floor near the bed, so he knew he really had used it. If Sarah mentioned the encounter, he'd just pass it off as a side effect of Sophie's psychic ability, that maybe she'd imagined it. Perhaps he'd tell her the truth someday, but right now he didn't want to add to Sarah's stress.

At five-fifteen he was at her door. He'd gone to the place they used to eat, near his old apartment. She recognized the bright red containers immediately.

"Cool. I haven't eaten there in at least a year. Love their kung pao."

"I remembered, so that's what I got. And lo mein for Sophie."

At the sound of her name, Sophie came to the kitchen and pulled a chair back from the table. She climbed up and leaned over the containers, sniffing. "Smells good, Mamma."

"You can thank Mr. Chris, honey. He knows what we like."

She gave him a smile as Sophie said, "Thank you Mr. Chris." His heart began to melt and turned to pudding when Sophie slipped from her chair to hug him around the waist, her head barely touching his elbow.

"You're welcome, Miss Sophie. Oh, I got something for you."

Her eyes lit up when she saw the plastic tiny panda figure he handed her. Her gap-toothed grin was adorable, as she played with the panda at the table. "They sold those at the counter," he explained to Sarah. "And these are for you." He handed her a bright red box of matches, with a gold-embossed tiger on it. The drop of her jaw amused him.

"You remembered!"

"How could I forget?"

Her arms came around him and he held on, enjoying the scent of her hair. He recalled she collected matches, a habit that had come in handy in an unexpected way, years before.

It reminded him of how much they had been through together, so giving her the matches was a tribute to that. One more method of trying to win her heart not with words but with deeds.

The meal was as good as he remembered, and they even had almond cookies for dessert. As they were cleaning up the plates, Sophie went to wash up. It was then Sarah's voice took on a serious tone.

"I had a long talk with Wes today."

He stiffened, an involuntary reaction. Would he ever hear that guy's name and not cringe? "You did? Is he still in one piece?"

She smirked and ignored his question. "He apologized for the bar incident. He really can be nice, when he wants to be. He does seem genuinely interested in Sophie, and has invited us to go to his parent's house in Denver tomorrow night. Some sort of family get-together."

"Are you going?"

She kept moving, wiping down the table. He sensed she was trying to be nonchalant, but must be having strong feelings about meeting the family of her baby's father. "I'm considering it. If Sophie ends up having any relationship with him, his family will likely be involved. I need to know what kind of people they are."

"Makes sense."

That was one thing he loved about her—she was always logical, practical. He couldn't shake the sense, though, that she and Sophie may end up getting hurt. Jealousy wasn't his style, but he couldn't help but resent the role Wes had, but probably didn't appreciate. For better or worse, he'd be forever connected to Sarah because of Sophie. Chris longed to be in his position, and wondered if the man would ever realize how blessed he was.

Sarah hung the dishtowel on the oven door handle, and turned to him. "I know this can't be easy for you. Things are just complicated for me right now."

"I know. Just be careful. I don't trust that guy."

"You don't know him."

"No, but do you really know him either? You never dated him, it was just a fling, right? A guy like that won't suddenly change and become the ideal boyfriend, much less a doting father for a little girl." Her eyes warned him he had gone too far, but his concern for her overrode his tact. If she was in denial about what Wes was really like, he might take advantage of her. Again.

"No, we never spent much time together. But that doesn't change the fact he's here now."

"So am I."

He pulled her to him, devouring her mouth with his own. Words still weren't enough, and he needed her like a drug. Her arms came around his neck, and she kissed him back, making a small sound of desire. His arousal became evident and he pressed against her, backing her up against the counter. Her fingers were entwined in his hair. She pulled him to her hard, and he felt her teeth against his tongue. His need for her was crashing over him in tidal-wave fashion, but somewhere in his mind he knew he had to stop. She pulled her lips away from his, her breath ragged.

"We have to stop. Sophie…"

He was kissing his way down her neck. "I know…God, Sarah, I can't take it much longer...I need you."

Pushing on his chest with her hands, she brought him back to cold reality. She slipped away from him just as Sophie returned to the kitchen.

"Mamma, can I watch cartoons?"

"Sure, hon. Mr. Chris and I are going to do some more packing."

Still panting, he stood there in the kitchen. The heat between his legs was dissipating, his heart returning to a normal beat. The craving, the need…that wasn't going away anytime soon, if ever.

~*~

Sarah was relieved, but also disappointed when Chris finally left. Relieved because the torture of having him near was becoming unbearable. He looked so good, better than in her memories. With his shorter hair and clean-shaven face, it was like having a new and improved version of the man who had once stolen her heart, not to mention how he'd often made her moan in ecstasy.

It was the ecstasy part she couldn't stop thinking about. She'd been tempted to take him to her bedroom and shut the door while Sophie watched television, but her conscience had taken over. They kept finding excuses to bump into each other, staying in excruciatingly close proximity. So it was a relief when he said goodnight, but then a sadness descended as she closed the door.

She'd been so distracted with the business with Wes, and everything else going on, she couldn't even think about what to do with Chris. Her resolve was weakening every time she saw him, and her desire to get him naked was turning into a need. What kind of a fool would she be to turn him away and never see him again?

One who would never know if we could still make magic.

As she locked up the house for the night and set out her clothes for the morning, a fantasy began to spin in her mind. She'd show up at his door, in nothing but her raincoat. Or maybe some sexy lingerie underneath. He'd carry her to the bed and undress her slowly, then worship her with kisses everywhere. She'd climb on top of him, and he'd take her to that awesome place, somewhere between their bodies and their souls.

The images faded away as she went to tuck Sophie in. Her room was littered with half-open boxes. It seemed that every time they'd packed her toys away, she had a sudden need for one, and they'd have to dig through them again. Sitting on her daughter's bed, she pulled the covers up under the girl's chin.

"Listen, Missy. We've got a long day ahead of us tomorrow, so you need to get some sleep tonight. No dream-walking, okay?"

"Okay, Mamma. But what if Mr. Chris comes back?"

She didn't know what that had to do with her dream episodes, but it pleased her she seemed to like him.

"He won't be back for a few days. Tomorrow we are going to Mr. Wes's house, to meet his family. They live in Denver, so we'll be up late tomorrow night."

"Is Mr. Chris your boyfriend or is Mr. Wes?"

She paused, not knowing whether to laugh or be worried. A five-year old shouldn't be asking such things, but Sophie wasn't typical. "Neither one. They're just my friends. But Mr. Chris and I used to be boyfriend and girlfriend, a long, long time ago."

"Oh. Then he must love you."

Her heart skipped a beat just then. Did he? She'd been so caught up with the physical longing for him that had resurfaced, she hadn't thought about how they felt emotionally. Or had she been avoiding it?

She didn't answer, but Sophie's eyes were drooping and she yawned. Sarah moved the blonde curls aside and kissed her daughter's forehead. "Time to get some sleep, Sophie."

Back in her own room, she went through her closet, looking for a box. Buried underneath a pile of clothes was a stationery box filled with letters from her college days. She went through it, searching for a particular letter, one she hadn't opened since it was sealed in 1978.

But it wasn't there. Wracking her brain, she tried to recall where it may have been stashed. It was an account of her time with Chris, written when she believed they had broken up, shortly after they first met. It had been cathartic to purge all of her feelings and memories of that time, and recount everything that had happened. She'd even detailed their psychic-sexual experience together. When he returned a few days later and they were together again, she had hidden the sealed letter away.

When they parted for good less than a year later, she'd already moved a few times, and again after Sophie was born. So there was no telling where the letter was now. Being with Chris again had triggered her memory, and she wanted to read the letter, which included a description of how it felt the first time they had made love, the first time they had astral projected together, melding their minds as closely as their bodies. Maybe if she could read how it once felt, she'd know if it was worth the risk to have that connection with him once again.

A half-hour later, she gave up the search. She was tired of digging through the debris of her life, searching for a deeper meaning. Perhaps it was time to just go with the flow and let things play out.

~*~

Chris had been at his hotel so long, the desk clerks knew him by name. When at first he'd explained he was in town for Dr. Engle's funeral, they were kind enough to give him a discounted rate, except for Saturday night. He was grateful for any help he could get at the moment. This trip was already costing him more than he'd expected. As he passed the counter, the perky, dark-haired girl greeted him with three folded notes in her hand.

"Good evening, Mr. Levine. There's a few messages for you."

"Thanks, Becky. Guess I'm popular tonight."

"I don't doubt it, sir. Have a great evening. Let me know if you need anything, okay?"

"Will do. You have a good one."

As he walked away, he realized one of them had her name and phone number on it. He smiled over his shoulder and she winked. She couldn't be much older than twenty, and though she was attractive, he had someone else setting him on fire at the moment. He could still taste Sarah's kiss on his lips, feel her touch on his skin. As he reached the elevator, he tossed Becky's note in a trash can.

Damn. It really must be love this time.

The other two were both from a Mr. Reinhold, a manager at the bank holding his mortgage. "Urgent he speak with you as soon as possible" was underlined, indicating the man had been insistent.

There was nothing to tell the guy, other than the condo hadn't sold yet, and he didn't have enough money to get caught up. Chris glanced at his watch. It was almost nine at night, so even with the time difference, the bank would be closed. He'd just have to stall them as long as he could. He'd call his realtor tomorrow and see if they could lower the asking price, though it killed him to do it again.

His earlier euphoria from his make out session with Sarah was dissipating. His insides clenched at the thought of her going out with Wes again. He was putting everything aside for the hope she would agree to be with him, yet here he was, still hanging on like a fish on her line. He understood her reasoning for what she was doing, but it didn't make it any easier to bear being pushed to the background. He was putting everything else in his life in jeopardy in order to accommodate her, with no guarantee of success.

But she hadn't asked him to do any of that, so he had nothing else to blame but his own foolish heart. He flipped on the television, and sat back on the empty bed. He was running out of time and options. He couldn't stop her from going to Denver to meet Wes's family, and he understood her need to go there. But if she was still undecided after that, if she couldn't admit she wanted him and loved him, that they still had a chance to be happy together, then he would have his answer.

He'd have to let her go.

13 The Party

The next evening, Wes was late. Sarah and Sophie were sitting on Zac's front steps waiting. Amanda sat on a bean bag chair on the front porch, and Zac was walking Frodo around the yard on a leash.

"Seems like that pup has just about grown into his big, hairy feet," Sarah remarked, watching Sophie as she went to pet the dog. "He must be part St. Bernard."

Amanda laughed. "You might be right. I hope he doesn't get much bigger. If he eats more than he does now, I'm buying stock in a dog food company."

Sarah stood, pacing the walk. "Where is Wes? It's quarter to six already."

Zac had wandered over. She was still annoyed at him for the bar incident, but knew he meant well. He always did, even though he might not say as much. "Are you nervous, McKenn? You shouldn't be. Probably a snooty bunch, given where they live."

"I'm not nervous. Well, maybe a little. Not for me, but for Sophie."

"She'll be all right. Kids don't think like we do."

"Maybe you're right." She said the words, but she wasn't sure. Her intuition was ringing alarm bells at her all day, but she figured she was just being paranoid. If during the evening she or Sophie were uncomfortable, she'd simply ask Wes to bring them home. It was less than two hours' drive, and he'd agreed to bring them home whenever she wanted, so she really needed to relax and just go with it.

Ten minutes later, he showed up, unapologetic. It rankled her, but she'd already committed. She went to hug Amanda goodbye.

"Have fun you two…ahhh." With a sharp intake of breath, Amanda pulled from Sarah's embrace. Her hands went to her stomach, and she winced.

"Are you in pain?" Sarah asked, realizing the answer before Amanda even nodded. There was a tense silence while everyone stared, waiting. Soon she straightened, blowing out a long breath.

"False alarm," she said, her smile returning. "Lil' bugger does this lately. Guess he or she is getting anxious to join us."

"You know, they have a test now where you can see the baby and they'll tell you the gender. Didn't do it when I was pregnant, but maybe it'd be nice to know."

Amanda patted her belly, still breathing deep. "Zac wanted to, but I still like surprises."

Zac was now at her side, and as he helped his wife up the stairs he said over his shoulder, "Drive careful. Don't be too late, you guys."

They disappeared into the house and Wes opened the back door of his BMW for Sophie. He strapped her in as Sarah settled in the front seat, and then they were off, heading south out of Fort Winston.

Sophie entertained herself with a book she had brought, and by looking out the window. They'd been to Denver only a few times since she'd moved to Fort Winston, and Sarah enjoyed the old familiar sights and sounds of the drive down. As always, there was a pang of sadness when they passed the exit which led to the house she'd grown up in, but she pushed it aside. It was easy to do, with Wes's constant chatter to distract her.

She'd gone along, nodding and answering, but her mind was elsewhere. She wondered what Chris was doing. He hadn't called, not that she'd had any time to talk. She'd even worked through lunch so she could leave early to get ready for the party, only to have to wait around for Wes.

When they turned onto Wes's street, she had a hard time keeping her mouth closed. She wanted to gape in awe at the elegant houses, framed by elaborate gardens and wrought iron gates. Two such gates welcomed them at the Porter home, gliding open after Wes punched a number on a keypad embedded in one of the stone pillars at the entrance.

"Wow," escaped her lips as they approached the house. It was a mansion, all brick and rock and carved wood. He parked the car at the edge of the circular driveway, and came around to open both of their doors. Sarah stepped onto the brick walkway, after Sophie took her hand.

"Look, Mamma, the trees have shapes."   Several hedges were shaped into animals, lending a whimsical touch to the impressive gardens.

"That's called a topiary," Wes explained. "I used to watch Alberto, our gardener, shape them. Sometimes he'd let me pick which animal he'd do."

Sophie smiled at that, putting Sarah at ease. They followed Wes up the wide stone steps to a huge double door of carved wood. Stained glass framed both sides of the door, and above the transom. *We are seriously out of our league here. I feel like Alice about to go down the rabbit hole...*

He pushed open the door to a tiled entryway. A chandelier hung from the ceiling far above, catching the last rays of the sun as they filtered through the stained glass. A polished wood bannister edged the wide stairway in front of them, which curved up to the second level. A tiny woman in a blue uniform entered the foyer and welcomed Wes with a grin.

"Everyone is out back, Mr. Wesley."

He turned a bit pink at the use of his formal name, but thanked the woman and gestured for Sarah and Sophie to precede him. They walked through three rooms, each more grand than the one before it. "I couldn't even afford one of these chairs, let alone the rest of this furniture." Sarah meant to say it under her breath, but Wes heard.

"My mom was an interior decorator, once upon a time. So don't be intimidated. She gets carried away sometimes."

His mother was the first to greet them as they stepped through French doors onto a wide brick patio. Tables and chairs were everywhere, covered in white linen and lit with soft candles. It looked like an outdoor bistro in France, or what Sarah imagined one would look like. Crystal goblets and vases stuffed with fresh flowers adorned every table, and the scent of something delicious filled the air.

"Welcome to our home." Wes's mother extended a delicate bejeweled hand in her direction. Sarah shook it, noting how soft the woman's skin was. Her blonde hair was short, and teased high on her head, with little flips at the end, as though she was still stuck in the 'sixties. Her lipsticked smile was polished, professional. Her pale blue eyes held a warmth, for a moment. Then she looked past them as though awaiting the next guest.

Wes didn't seem to notice his mother's inattention and made the introductions, donning his gentlemanly role once again. "Mother, may I present my friend, Ms. Sarah McKenn, and her daughter, Miss Sophie."

Sarah stiffened at the word, 'friend', though she couldn't imagine him introducing her any other way. 'Mother of my long-lost daughter' might be a shock for the woman, after all. "Pleased to meet you, Mrs. Porter," she said, instead of what she was thinking.

Looking back at her, Mrs. Porter smiled again. "Call me Nancy." She gestured toward the tables. "Please, do sit down. The buffet is over there. We'll be having cake promptly at nine."

With that, she proffered her cheek for her son to kiss, and went to greet more guests who had just arrived. Sarah felt a bit bewildered, and looked to Wes, who shrugged his shoulders and led them to a table. Sarah set down her purse and they walked to the buffet, which was overflowing with food. "This is a little family get-together? I can't imagine what a real party is like for you folks."

Wes shrugged again, handing her a plate. "Those we usually hold at a hotel. Easier to clean up."

Shaking her head, she went down the line, helping Sophie fill her plate, and putting a spoonful of everything on her own.

Whatever the outcome, at least tonight they wouldn't go hungry.

The rest of the evening was spent at their table. She was grateful for the excellent champagne, which helped to ease her nerves. There were about fifty people on the patio, all friends and family, and though they were polite, none were very friendly. She and Sophie sat on the sidelines, taking it all in. She'd known Wes came from a well-to-do background, but she'd had no idea how wealthy his family really was. She found herself searching for traces of her daughter in them— at least, physically. She was able to pick out Wes's siblings from their looks alone before she was introduced. Something about the jawline and of course, the light hair, was familiar. Could Sophie sense it?

She looked to her daughter who alternated between watching the activity and picking at her food. *No, I'd know if she did, because she'd ask about it.*

After the birthday cake was served, Wes disappeared. Soon he returned with two young girls, one about Sophie's age and the other one a bit older. "These are my nieces, Jessica and Ashley. You can go upstairs to play for a while, if you like."

The girls looked at Sophie with placid faces, seemingly uninterested. Then the taller one said, "C'mon. I brought my Jem dolls. I'll show you."

Sophie followed the other girls, and Wes went to talk to someone at another table. Sarah sat back, sipping her champagne and listening to the soft music that played from speakers set in the wall of the house. When the song changed, she recognized Sade's smoky voice; it seemed the Porters had good taste in music, too. Wes's sister, Cynthia, walked past, whispering to another woman and giggling. He had introduced her to Sarah earlier, and, like her mother, the woman was polite and polished. She'd welcomed Sarah and Sophie, thanked them for coming to the party, and then they were dismissed as she turned her attention to the next guest.

As Sarah looked around at the people, she began to feel more awkward, not less. Wes knew everyone of course, and had introduced her, but they all seemed to look through her as though she wasn't really there. Or like they knew she wouldn't be around for long, so there was no point in engaging.

Because I'm of a lower class? Because I'm a single mother? Or because of Wes's habits?

Questions swirled in her head. It wasn't that she cared whether or not they approved of her or liked her, but she wanted to know why, exactly. She was used to not fitting in, but she usually knew the reason.

"Would you like some more champagne, Sarah?" Wes was back, and he signaled the server without waiting for her response. *How many people did they employ, just for a party?*

"No thanks, I'd just like some water please."

By the time the young man brought her a bottle of Perrier, her head was swimming. Too much rich food, too much champagne. Not something she was used to. The occasional glass of wine and a pizza—that was more her style. She needed to find the bathroom and splash some cold water on her face. She took a long sip of the fizzy water and stood slowly. "I'll be right back. I need to find the restroom."

Wes pulled her chair out for her. "The house has six bathrooms, one is bound to be unoccupied."

She wandered into the house, and found that the closest bathroom was indeed occupied. So she took to the stairs, hoping to peek in on Sophie if she could find where the girls were playing. Lights were on in nearly every room, and she marveled again at the décor, a mix of Old World and Contemporary, that somehow worked. Mrs. Porter did have some flair with interior design.

She made it to the second floor bathroom, just as the door closed. She kept walking down the long hallway, to a bedroom with the door ajar. She was planning to slip in and use the bathroom without anyone knowing, but as she reached the door, she heard a woman mention Wes's name. She froze, and the conversation continued, loud enough for her to hear every word.

"Oh, come on, Felicia. Don't tell me you still have a crush on my brother."

The other woman giggled, and asked if her lipstick was too dark. Having gained the necessary approval, she added, "But I am curious about the girl he's with."

Sarah looked around to be sure no one saw her standing just outside the door. Confident she was undetected, she trained her ears to the women's voices.

Cynthia snorted. "Just the flavor of the week, I'm sure. You know how Wes is. He's got another new toy."

Felicia's voice was more serious. "Yeah, but she's got a kid. Maybe he's maturing, dating single moms now."

Sarah almost snorted at that. *If these two only knew....*

Cynthia's voice was flat, with a hint of annoyance. "I can't even get him to do anything with my two, and they're his nieces. He can't stand kids. He's one himself."

It wasn't anything she hadn't already considered but she almost felt bad for Wes. If his own family felt that way about him...

Cynthia continued her observations. "And come on, that mousy little thing, in her department store clothes? Guarantee you she's just a piece of ass to him. So you may have a chance after all, darling."

Both women laughed, their voices coming closer. Sarah ducked down the hall and into the now vacant bathroom, shutting the door just as the two emerged from the bedroom. She fell back against the door, tears of humiliation threatening. She looked at her reflection in the mirror, wishing she'd worn a better outfit. If she'd had a better outfit, she would have.

Who cares? Would it have helped?

Humiliation turned to anger. *They know nothing about us. Not exactly the people I want to hang with, either.*

Splashes of cold water on her face did help, and soon she returned to the party. Sophie was at the table, looking forlorn.

"Honey, are you okay? Did you have fun with the girls?"

"Yes. They let me watch."

Sarah took her daughter's hand. "They wouldn't let you play?"

Sophie nodded. A glance at her watch told Sarah it was after ten, and she felt no compelling reason to stay. She'd had enough. Spotting Wes at another table, she rose to tell him she wanted to get going. He saw her and motioned her over.

"Sarah, come meet my father."

He was a tall man, with thinning sandy hair that must have been as blond as Wes's at one time. Fit and tanned, with the same perfect smile as his son. *He's a dentist. Of course he has great teeth.*

"Don Porter. Nice to meet you, Sarah."

Taking his hand, she inclined her head toward her daughter. "And that's Sophie. Thanks for having us. It's been lovely. But I think we'd better get going, Wes."

It took Wes another ten minutes to make his exit from the party, chatting with this person and that, while Sarah and Sophie stood waiting by the door. When at last they were in the BMW and traveling away from the grand house, Wes said, "That went well. Everyone loved you and Sophie. I knew they would."

She wondered how on earth someone could be so clueless.

14 The Offer

Sarah waited until Sophie was asleep on the backseat before she responded to Wes's assessment of the evening. "Thanks again for inviting us. Your family was nice, and your home's beautiful. But I don't think we really fit in."

He shot her a look in the darkened car. "Why do you think that? They all liked you, I could tell."

She hesitated, knowing his view of his family was far apart from hers. "I'm not so sure. I mean, they were polite, but…it felt awkward, like they didn't know what to make of us. And your sister…" She instantly regretted bringing it up, but her anger over Cynthia's attitude still simmered.

"What did Cynth say this time? She's always on my case about something."

"I overheard her when I was looking for the bathroom. She thinks I'm just your 'flavor of the week'."

He laughed, but there was an undertone of annoyance. "Well, it doesn't matter what she thinks, or any of them, for that matter. They'll come to know you in time. In fact, I was thinking maybe you and Sophie could move into the guest house. My dad could probably recommend you for a job in Denver, he knows everyone. When I'm not traveling for work, then we can do stuff together, like be a family, you know?"

The urge to gape was back again but she kept her mouth shut. He couldn't be serious…could he?

"Wes, I don't think…I'm glad you want to help, but we're still moving to Arizona in a matter of days. I already have a job waiting for me there."

They were turning onto her street; it was almost midnight, and this night was nearly over. Wes didn't seem perturbed by her rejection, and continued his description of a perfect life.

"You wouldn't even have to work, I make good money. You'll both have the best clothes, you can go shopping all you want. My mom and sister have great taste, I'm sure they'd love to help. And Sophie could go to school nearby. Maybe even a private school, like I did."

The mention of his sister brought her humiliation back full force. And if he thought she would play the pampered housewife type, he really didn't understand her at all. She had no interest in this picture of life he was painting.

When he pulled the car up to the curb, she didn't wait for him to come around to open the door. She jumped out and opened the back door, and as she lifted her daughter from the seat, Wes took the sleeping girl and carried her to Sarah's door. It wasn't until she reached in her purse for her key that she noticed a note taped to the front door. Her heart began pounding; a note this late at night could not be good news. She moved under the porch light so she could read it.

"They're at the hospital. It's Amanda." She looked up at Wes, still holding Sophie in his arms.

"Let's go. I'll take you."

As they hurried back to the car, her earlier annoyance with Wes began to ease. He didn't hesitate to help, as late as it was and with the long drive would have to get home. He was a decent guy, but she was still uncomfortable with the scenario he had described, about living at his house. The question that gnawed at her was, would it be a better opportunity for Sophie?

Her thoughts continued as they raced toward the hospital. His was a big family, maybe some among them would be kind. Sophie's education would be top notch. She'd never again have to worry about her daughter going without. At the very least, maybe Wes would help out with their finances, even if they didn't stay in Colorado.

There would be time enough to discuss it later. There was so much to consider but right now, Amanda and Zac needed her.

~*~

Chris put down the magazine, wondering what he was going to do now that he'd read the last one. The table next to his uncomfortable chair in the hospital waiting room had been littered with old magazines, mostly women's publications about gardening and family menus. He'd spent the past few hours leafing through them, in between rounds of pacing the hall. Zac hadn't been out of Amanda's room to give him an update in at least forty minutes. How long did it take to have a baby, anyway?

He thought with some irritation that Sarah should have been home by now and got the note Zac had left on her door. It was well past midnight. He thought of driving over to be sure she saw the note, but if she wasn't home yet, then what? He'd feel silly waiting on her doorstep like some lost puppy.

He stood up to stretch. Maybe another cup of coffee would help. He'd get one for Zac, who probably needed some as well. He'd stopped by to see them at home earlier, because he just couldn't spend another night in his room alone. He'd brought a bucket of chicken and offered to keep them company, since Sarah and Sophie were out for the evening. Zac had laughed and said something about Chris being "whipped". Amanda said she was glad to have someone for Zac to hang out with while she went to lie down. She was having pains then, but insisted it was going to pass. The baby wasn't due for another few weeks, at least. But by the time he was about to leave, around ten, she was concerned enough to ask Zac to take her to the hospital. The pains weren't easing, but intensifying, and becoming more frequent. He followed them over and by the time Zac was helping her out of the car, her water had broken and she was in full-blown labor.

Her parents had arrived at the hospital shortly after Zac brought Amanda in. Her mother, Peggy Bresky, was now with Amanda in her room, and her father, Victor, was asleep in a nearby chair, snoring. Chris had promised to wake him if anything happened.

As he dug in his pockets for some change for the vending machine, Sarah appeared in the hallway with Sophie in tow, and Wes Porter right behind them.

"Chris! What are you—how did you know about Amanda?" She was out of breath and her face was flushed. Sophie looked sleepy, but curious, looking up with half-opened eyes and disheveled hair.

"I stopped by their place earlier, and she wasn't feeling well then. It got worse, so we brought her here. I guess she's in labor."

Sarah looked at Wes, then back at him. "Will you guys watch Sophie for a minute? I've got to see her."

"Sure," Chris said, extending a hand to Sophie. As Sarah released her hand, Sophie took his hand, and Wes moved in to hold Sophie's other hand. He gave Chris a look that hinted of challenge, but Sarah was already walking away and didn't see the two men leading her daughter to a nearby chair.

"I'm thirsty," Sophie said in a small voice.

"I'll get her some water," Wes announced, as though he was saving her from some great threat, and strode off to find a cup.

"Are you sleepy, Sophie? Or hungry?"

"I slept in the car. My tummy's still full from dinner."

He smiled at the way her voice was so child-like, but her tone and demeanor was so grown-up. She seemed to be wise beyond her years, but he couldn't explain why that was so. It was just a sense he had about her. "Oh, good. Well, tell me if you need anything."

She was quiet for a moment, and then asked, "Is Amanda having the baby now?"

"We'll see. It takes time sometimes." He found a children's magazine, one of the ones he had skipped, and handed it to her. She began looking through it, and Wes appeared with a cup in hand.

Once Sophie was settled, Wes sat opposite them on a chair. Mr. Bresky was still asleep, his head leaning precariously to one side. Hospital staff came and went, and the minutes ticked by. Wes picked up a magazine, pretending to read, but Chris noticed the man watching him, and trying to do so unnoticed. "If you've got something to say, Porter, say it."

His blue eyes feigned innocence, followed by a smug smile. "Not much to say to you, my friend. Except you can't seem to take a hint, can you?"

"And you can?"

"She's moved on from her past, buddy. I'm here to stay, whether you like it or not."

"Well, my presence here is up to her, not you. So there's no point in discussing it."

It was a struggle to keep his tone casual. He was aware of Sophie sitting next to him, engrossed in her magazine. He knew she could still hear everything, but he couldn't take Wes outside at the moment to have a real discussion. Probably just as well, he thought, his hand clenching into an involuntary fist.

Wes sat back with a grin, putting his hands behind his head. "You're right, there's nothing to discuss. But you better start packing your bags, dude, because it's already been decided. She knows they'll both be taken care of with me, in the finest style. She'll never have to worry about anything."

His gut felt as though Wes had punched him with a fist, not just with words. *Already decided? That fast? He's lying. He has to be.*

He wanted to run to Sarah and ask if it was true. She'd only spent the evening with his family. *One evening!* But if they were as wealthy as Zac had said, she might be tempted, for Sophie's sake. He tried to gulp in a breath, without being obvious. His pulse was hammering, his palms sweating. He wiped them on his jeans, and stood up. "I was going to get some coffee when you guys came in. You want some?"

Wes had picked up the magazine again, and was pretending to read, yawning. "No, thanks. I'll watch the kid."

The kid. Nice way to describe his daughter. His irritation at Wes's flippant attitude toward Sophie was almost enough to keep him in his seat, but he needed to talk to Sarah. Looking back to be sure the girl was okay, he walked casually toward the vending machine. Once he'd filled two paper cups, he moved down the hallway toward Amanda's room.

The door was cracked, and he hesitated before entering. He really wanted to talk to Sarah alone for a minute. He could hear Mrs. Bresky talking to Zac about getting some food. As her voice came closer, Chris ducked around the corner. She and Zac walked from the room in the other direction, likely in search of something to eat. He'd brought the coffee for Zac, but maybe he could use it to get Sarah out of the room for a moment so they could talk. He paused outside the door again, hearing Sarah's voice.

"They'll only be gone for a few minutes, and I have to tell you something."

When she answered, Amanda sounded more chipper than he expected for a woman in labor. "The pain meds haven't totally kicked in yet, but if I start to sound loopy, you'll know why. So tell me about tonight."

"Well, it was awkward. I don't think we fit in at all. But they have a beautiful house.'"

Were they nice to you, though? Did you like them?"

"They were nice, I guess, just not very welcoming. Polite, but distant. Of course, they didn't know anything about Sophie being his daughter, but still…anyway, the big news is Wes wants us to move in there. He wants to take care of us."

His hands shook, nearly spilling the coffee. *That bastard was telling the truth.*

Amanda was quiet for a moment, then groaned. "Sorry, Lil' bugger doesn't like to be ignored. Ouch. So, what are you going to do?"

"I told him we're still leaving town. But then, I wondered if maybe…it would be better for Sophie if we stayed?"

He'd heard enough. The indecision in her voice told him everything he needed to know. The punched feeling in his gut moved to his chest, making it hard to breathe. He found a nearby restroom and poured the coffee down the sink, watching it swirling down the drain along with his hopes. He took a long look in the mirror, at the fool who'd almost turned his life upside down for a woman, once again. Another woman who had her priorities, none of which involved him.

When he entered the waiting room, Zac was there with Mrs. Bresky, who was sharing a vending-machine sandwich with her now-awake husband. Chris said his farewells, and promised to stop by the next day to check on them, and to find out about the baby. He didn't mention that he hadn't said goodbye to Sarah.

Because saying goodbye to Sarah was something he'd never wanted, never even imagined, so he had no idea how of how to go about it.

~*~

Nurses and technicians kept coming in the room every few minutes, which made it difficult to finish her conversation with Amanda. Then there were the long pauses where she held her friend's hand while the contractions took over. Memories of when she gave birth to Sophie came flooding back, and she knew the worst was yet to come. "That's it, just breathe…you're doing great, Mandy."

When Amanda finally sat back on her pillow, and began to breathe normally again, her first words were, "Okay, so where were we? Oh, yeah, moving to Denver, maybe?"

Sarah picked up a cloth and dabbed Amanda's forehead. Her russet hair was matted to her face, which was still pink from the exertion. "I did think about it for, a minute or two. But that's not us. His family's lifestyle is so far beyond what we're used to. And I don't want to be beholden to him, you know? What if we live there and we hate it? I want Sophie to have the best, but I doubt I'd be happy, so how could I help her then?"

"Makes sense. I understand your desire to stay independent. But, since he's her father, he should bear some responsibility."

"Technically, yes. But I have a feeling there'd be some sticky strings attached."

"Probably. Plus, there's the fact that you already have strong ties to someone else."

Sarah felt her cheeks flush. Was it that obvious? She'd been surprised to see Chris at the hospital, but the fact that he stayed made her respect and affection for him increase tenfold. He really had been persistent and dependable since he'd come back, two things she'd once thought he lacked. Maybe he'd really had a change of heart.

"I know. I'm afraid I've neglected him, with all this drama going on with Wes. Chris told me he's willing to move to Arizona to be with me—with us—if that's what it takes. I didn't believe him at first."

"Honey, I don't know the guy like you do, but I can tell he's in love. Like he's never fell out of love, type of love. Ooooohh....ugh."

She grabbed her belly with both hands, her face twisted with pain. Another nurse came in, followed by a doctor. Sarah gave Amanda's arm a squeeze. "I'll go get your mom. Hang in there, Mandy."

She hurried to the waiting room, anxious to see Chris. The imminent arrival of a new life in the world, the child of her dearest friends, made her recall what was most important in her own life. She loved Sophie with all her heart, and wanted to provide a safe, loving environment for her child. Living with Wes and his family might be safe, but she knew in her heart it would not be a life filled with love.

But with Christian Levine it could be. He was the only man she'd ever truly loved. He was her soul mate, just as she'd known he was so many years ago, and she couldn't wait to tell him.

15 The Parting

When she got to the waiting room, Chris was gone. Amanda's mother looked at her expectantly, as though awaiting her cue. It was sweet and funny how excited both of Amanda's parents were for the arrival of their first grandchild, and Sarah was happy to deliver the news Mrs. Bresky was waiting to hear. "Peggy, Mandy needs you. The doctor just went in."

The petite redhead nearly knocked over her six-foot tall husband in her haste to reach her daughter. "Grandma Peggy's on her way. Thanks, sweetie."

She squeezed Sarah's arm as she passed. Turning to Zac, who was about to follow his mother-in-law, Sarah asked, "Where's Chris?"

"He left a few minutes ago. Not sure why, but he seemed in a hurry."

Sophie was in one of the chairs, asleep, in what looked like an uncomfortable position. Wes was nearby, oblivious to Sophie's discomfort. What had she expected?

She blew out a breath to hide her irritation. It was time to get her daughter home and into bed, but she had to do something first. "Wes, watch Sophie for a minute, please? I'll be right back."

He had nodded, so she hurried to the lobby, through the front doors and to the parking lot. No sign of Chris. She craned her neck to see, scanning over the lot, but saw no one, and no cars were moving.

He left without saying goodbye. Guess I deserve that. I'll call him in the morning.

Back in the waiting room, she told Mr. Bresky they were leaving. "Have to get Sophie to bed, and I've got work in the morning…oh, Amanda usually watches her…"

"I'm sure Peggy'll be glad to babysit. You remember where we live, don't you?"

"Yes, I do. Are you sure it won't be any trouble?"

Victor took her hand in his. "You've been there for Mandy many times. It's the least we can do."

"Great. I'll bring her by around eight-thirty then. Thanks. Hug Peggy for me."

Wes already had Sophie in his arms, and they walked to the car in silence. When they were leaving the parking lot, she glanced back at the hospital. "I hope everything goes well for her."

Wes answered, not looking at her. "Me, too, though I know nothing about how that stuff goes."

Exhaustion was setting in. She hadn't slept well in what seemed like weeks. Worrying about the baby coming early didn't help, but she was glad that at least this way she'd get to be part of it, and Sophie would, too.

Wes seemed tired, he hadn't said much during the drive to her house. She toyed with the idea of letting him sleep on her sofa instead of driving back to Denver, but then she'd never get any sleep. She wouldn't put it past him to try to seduce her in the middle of the night, and she didn't have the strength at the moment to deal with the aftermath of rejecting him again.

Once Sophie was tucked into bed, she entered the kitchen to find Wes peering into the fridge. When he saw her, he wiggled his eyebrows suggestively. "I thought you might have some wine, so we could relax and unwind. But no luck."

"Wes, I have to get to bed. I work tomorrow. Thanks for everything, though. I really do appreciate it."

She took his arm and was leading him to the door, when he grasped her arms and turned her toward him. His denim-blue eyes, so much like Sophie's, almost made her feel some sympathy. But her instincts told her there was no future with him, so she pulled away.

"Sarah, I want to stay here with you. Don't make me go."

Touching his cheek, she tried to be kind but firm. "I'm sorry. This isn't going to work, between you and me."

"Just kiss me. If you still want me to leave after that, I'll go."

He didn't wait for her agreement, but bent his head to his task. His lips were wide, sensual. He was technically skilled, using his lips and tongue in a manner that was designed to excite. But she felt nothing. As handsome and charming as Wes was, he never invoked that spark within her, that thrum of desire that made her heart beat erratically and her breath catch in her throat.

No, it was someone else who made her feel that way. The one she let slip away, when she should have held him tight.

The kiss ended, and Wes looked at her expectantly. She lowered her lashes, looking down, and he released her. "I'm sorry Wes. If you still want to keep in touch, because of So-phie—"

He moved toward the door, and turned abruptly at her words. "Do you know how many girls would kill to be in your shoes? To have *my* child, to be part of my world?" His eyes, so kind and full of desire a moment ago, now stared at her with menace, and a touch of hurt.

"I don't know, and I honestly don't care, Wes. I didn't choose to be in this situation."

"Well, neither did I, but I offered to help and this is how you thank me. You think that you, of all people, are too good for *me?* You think you can make it on your own, with a kid to support?"

He was nearly a foot taller than her, but she was about to punch him anyway. She held back on her urge, and her voice became deadly calm. "Yes, I do. I've been doing it for years. And if the condition for you helping your only daughter to have a good life is us living with you, then we'll have to pass. You have some growing up to do yourself, and I already have one child to raise. Now get out."

He threw open the door and stomped down the stairs. As she closed the door, she heard him shout, "It's him, isn't it? He left you once, he'll do it again!"

Falling against the closed door, she slid down to the floor. She hugged her knees and began to have a good, long cry.

~*~

At three in the morning, Chris finally lay down to sleep. He'd been on the phone for an hour, but he'd found a flight to New York the next evening. Sort of. He was on standby. With any luck, he'd make it to his parents' house late at night, and they'd be too tired to grill him on what had happened.

He'd spend a few days securing his new job, then fly back to California to get his car and his belongings out of the condo. Then, if it didn't sell in time, the bank could have it. He was tired of fighting the tidal wave of bad luck that was crashing over his life lately. Maybe if he just rode it out, he wouldn't get so battered.

At least all the planning kept his mind off Sarah. He'd already decided what he was going to do. He had a parting gift for her, a memento. He couldn't leave without saying what was in his heart. At least this time, he knew she would receive it, unlike his unacknowledged letters to her long ago.

The next morning, he was up early. Somehow, he felt a sense of purpose that kept him going despite the fatigue. He had breakfast at the old diner next to the motel where he'd first met Sarah. Memories returned, and he replayed the whole time period in his mind, like a music video. Except this time, he knew it would be his last visit to Fort Winston. Once Sarah left, he'd have no reason to ever return.

Next he went to the hospital. Zac was holding vigil in Amanda's room, where she was sleeping. He rose from his chair with a finger to his lips, so Chris whispered, "Is everything okay?"

"She's fine, just tired. It's a boy."

He slapped Zac on the back. "A boy, huh? Congratulations."

The other man tugged on his goatee, pride evident in his wide smile. "Yep. He's healthy, but came a bit early. Tiny thing. They have him in an incubator. Just to make sure he's gonna be okay."

"I'm sure he will be. Have you named him yet?"

Zac moved closer to his wife's bed, watching her sleep. "Not yet. We have some ideas, but she was too tired to talk about it."

"I bet. Hey, can you give this to Sarah when you see her?"

He handed over a brown paper shopping bag, stapled together at the top. It wasn't an attractive gift package, but sturdy enough to hold the contents.

Zac held up his hands, not taking the bag. "Why don't you give it to her yourself? She's coming over on her lunch break."

How could he expect anyone else to understand? He didn't really understand it himself, how he lost her again. He had been determined to win her back this time, but now he knew that was impossible if she didn't want him in her life. "Naw. It's over, man. I can see that now. I have no right to come here and stir up her world. She has her plans, her priorities. Her daughter comes first, and I respect that."

"Yeah, but you should still talk to her. Just leaving like this…"

Fighting the lump that was forming and making it hard to talk, he set the bag on a chair. "Just see that she gets it. My plane leaves tonight, I have to go pack."

The disappointment in his new friend's eyes didn't make what he was doing any easier. So he added the real reason he was leaving. "I love her too much to interfere with her happiness."

Zac shook his hand. "Take care of yourself."

"You, too. And your new family."

As he walked down the hall, his steps were leaden. There was nothing left to fight for, and he had nothing much left to lose. He got to his rental car, drove away and didn't look back.

~*~

Sarah was tackled by Zac as soon as she entered Amanda's room. He folded her in a hug, saying, "It's a boy!"

Sarah returned the hug, winking at Amanda over his shoulder. "That's great. Congratulations, Dad."

Amanda was awake and holding her baby, the tiny bundle swaddled in a blanket. A nurse stood by, ready to take him away. "Wait just a minute?" Amanda asked the nurse. "My friend wants to meet him." Sarah moved to the bedside, and Amanda held him up so she could see. "Say hello to Ryan Zachary Daley."

"Oh, he's gorgeous…" His pink little face was a miniature version of Zac's, except for his upturned nose, which resembled Amanda's. His head was bald, but for a thin covering of dark hair. His eyes opened for a moment, looking straight at her, then closed again. "He looks sleepy."

Amanda handed him to the nurse. "Just had his lunch. Now I can have mine, maybe?"

The nurse agreed to send someone in with some food, and she took the newest member of the Daley family back to the Infant Care Unit. Sarah was close to tears, and she reached over to hug Amanda. "I'm so happy for you. You're going to be a great mom. Just ask Sophie."

"I would, but right now Sophie's being spoiled rotten by my mom. She's never going be the same, you know."

They laughed and talked for a few minutes, mostly about the rigors of childbirth. Then Zac asked, "Have you talked to Chris?"

"No, and I'm kind of worried. I called his room and left a message with the front desk, but never heard from him. Have you?"

She watched as husband and wife did that thing that couples do, where they look at each other and have whole conversations with just a glance. It only took a second but it told her something was up. Zac spoke first, handing her a brown paper shopping bag that had been in the corner of the room. "He's leaving town tonight. He asked me to give this to you."

"Did he say why he was leaving so soon, without seeing me?" Her fingers trembled as she ran them along the top of the bag. Lifting it, she felt the weight of something, and an image flashed in her mind. *It can't be. He'd never part with it.*

"Open the bag. Maybe he left a note?"

The staples holding the bag shut popped easily, and she caught them before they fell to the floor. Inside was a folded note, and the item she'd pictured—a large crystal. She pulled the crystal out, holding it up with both hands. A tear formed and she blinked it back. He was giving her something to remember him by, the crystal that had been such an important part of their psychic-sexual bonding. She knew he'd used it in his work with his out of body experiments, and it had to be one of his most prized possessions. So it was unthinkable he'd leave it to her. She looked at Zac, and saw pity in his dark eyes. She sensed he knew something more about this, but she would question him later. Placing the crystal back in the bag, she opened the note.

Sarah,

I'm sorry to leave like this without seeing you, but I've decided you were right. Getting too close and then having to part would hurt too much, and I never want to hurt you again. You have your daughter and her well-being to think of, and I was a fool to believe I could show up and expect you to change your plans to be with me. I guess it was wishful thinking, but I've had eight years to dream about it.

I'll never forget the most amazing experience of my life, which was the time I got to share with you. We will always be connected in that way.

Take care of yourself, and hug Sophie for me.

Love,
Chris

The note fluttered to the floor as she choked back a sob. Unable to stop them, she let the tears flow down her cheeks. Zac's arms came around her and Amanda said words of encouragement from her bed. She wallowed in her shock and sorrow a few moments, then pulled away. Finding a tissue in her purse, she dabbed her face.

"I was afraid he was going to do something like this. I realized last night that he's the best thing that ever happened to me, besides Sophie."

Zac picked up the note and tossed it in the bag. "So go get him, McKenn. He only left about a half hour ago. Said he still had to go to the hotel to pack and check out."

She looked to Amanda, who smiled and raised her eyebrow. "Unless you would rather move in with Wes?"

Zac shot Amanda a look of consternation, which almost made Sarah laugh. "No, I kicked him to the curb last night. Turns out he doesn't take rejection well."

"Big surprise."

Amanda pointed to the door. "Well, go then. Go get your man back."

Picking up the bag, Sarah blew them a kiss. "I love you guys."

Then she hurried to her car. She was on a mission to return the parting gift to its rightful owner, along with her heart.

16 The Promise

Sarah knocked on the door of room three-twenty-four. She was out of breath from running across the parking lot, carrying the bag with the crystal in it. The thing weighed at least ten pounds, and her purse alone was about half that. Her heart was beating frantically anyway, with the thought that she may be too late, and Chris would be gone.

When he opened the door, she froze. He stared at her, his mouth open in surprise. Then he looked at the bag in her hands. She held it out to him. "I'm here to return something that belongs to you. Well, two things, actually."

He took the bag from her, peeking inside. Then he tried to hand it back. "No, I want you to keep it." When she held her hands up to avoid taking it, he sighed. "So what's the other thing?"

Pressing herself up against him, she placed a hand on the back of his neck. "The other thing that belongs to you is *me.*"

He didn't resist, so she kissed him with all the passion and emotion that she'd been holding in check for way too long. He was still holding the bag, but he wrapped his free arm around her and backed his way into the room, taking her along with him. The door fell shut with a click, and they were alone.

Her purse had fallen to the floor along with the paper bag holding the crystal, so their hands were free, roaming over each other as though for the first time. She couldn't get enough of him, touching his face, grabbing hold of his hair. Now that she'd let her true feelings flow, it was impossible to stop.

While they kissed, his hands moved over her and his touch on her skin was electric. That thrumming of desire, that spark which had always been missing in her encounters with anyone else was pulsating through her now. He broke away from deep kissing her, and held her at arm's length. "I hope you know what you're doing, Sarah. If we do this, there's no turning back this time. I couldn't take losing you again."

"That's why I'm here. I don't want to lose you, either."

"But what about Wes? I thought you and he had…worked something out."

She placed a hand on his cheek. "Don't worry about him. Right now, I don't think he's ready to take on any responsibility as Sophie's father. He was expecting me to be with him, and when he realized that wasn't part of the deal, he turned against me. I don't need that kind of drama in my life, or around Sophie."

His hand closed over hers, and he kissed her fingers. "But he's still her father. That will never change."

"That's true, but we'll just have to find a way to deal with it."

Leaning her head onto his chest, she held him tight. "Chris, I'm sorry I pushed you aside through all this. I'm so used to handling everything on my own, plus it was all overwhelming. Seeing you again, dealing with Wes, us preparing to move, taking on a new job, and now Amanda having the baby…not to mention Sophie's strange dreams. It all piled up on me. But now, dealing with everything else seems easy compared to the prospect of never seeing you again."

He stroked her hair, and she could feel his heart beating in his chest. He was quiet for a moment, and she began to worry that maybe he'd changed his mind, and decided to leave anyway. When he spoke, her heart tugged at the hurt and longing she heard in his voice.

"Sarah, I've waited so long to hear you say you want me in your life, but I'm afraid to believe it. Afraid that I'll give up everything, and then you'll change your mind. I know you have Sophie to think of, and dreams of your own you want to fulfill. I don't want to be last on your list, I want to be your partner in life. I want to be by your side, not trailing behind."

"And I want you by my side, always. When I saw the crystal in that bag, I couldn't believe it. I never thought you'd part with it. I knew then you loved me, because you were willing to let me go if you thought that was what I truly wanted. But it's not. I want to be with you. I love you."

She looked into his sapphire eyes, and saw her love reflected back. "You know I love you. I've never stopped loving you."

His kiss was so thorough her knees buckled. In one movement he swept her off her feet, carrying her to the bed just as he had the first night they made love, years ago. Nothing about the way they touched and kissed, was new. It was all achingly familiar, and she reveled in how well she knew him. Knew where and how to touch him so his breath would catch; how to make him moan and bring him to the brink. He knew her most sensitive spots as well, and his hands were moving in the way they always had, slowly unbuttoning her blouse, while his lips were busy nipping at her ear, her neck. Sliding a finger inside her bra to tease a nipple, making her gasp. Not to be outdone, she slipped her fingers inside the waistband of his jeans, to fondle the dip between his cheeks, knowing how sensitive he was right there.

He pulled back from kissing her neck to ask, "Not that I want to stop, but don't you have to be at work?"

"I told them I needed a few hours. So you better take me now."

"Oh, I will. Let's get naked."

His shirt was unbuttoned in seconds, and thrown to the floor. He stood, undoing his jeans, and sliding them over his hips along with his underwear. Sarah's blouse and bra were also thrown to the pile, and she wiggled out of her dress slacks, kicking her sandals off in the process.

Chris took the crystal from the paper bag and set it on the table next to the bed. "Just like old times, eh?"

She smiled, unable to look away from the sight of him naked. He was fit and toned, his muscles well-defined, and she caught a glimpse of the tattoo on his back as he'd retrieved the crystal. She loved this man for his heart, his mind and his soul; the hot body was a bonus. He was a gentleman, too, pulling a condom from his suitcase, and rolling it onto the most delicious part of him, the part she wanted inside her. Now.

He was on top of her, nuzzling her neck again, pushing her thighs apart as he settled between them. A rush of wetness between her legs, so hot it surprised her, urged her on. Her hand slid between them to wrap around his cock, and she let out a gasp as she felt the heat of it against her palm. "Oh, God, Chris. I've missed you, missed this. I want you inside me so bad."

He needed no further prodding and moved forward, his length filling her in one thrust. Arching her body against his, she gripped his arms and her head fell back on the pillow. Colors swirled behind her closed lids, and that strange sense of euphoria came over her. She hadn't felt this way in years, but it came back to her so easily now. Her body was responding to his movements, but her mind was somewhere else, in another dimension. Her mental-self floated above their bodies, and she sensed his own mental being was with her, enveloping her. They were one, yet separate; he was making love to her mind and her body at the same time. She didn't know whether it was the crystal that caused it, or the soul-deep connection they had. All that mattered was their coupling, being as close as two humans could possibly be.

Pressing into her with an almost savage ferocity, his assault was causing waves of pleasure that radiated from deep inside her. Her breath came in gulps and sobs as it intensified, reaching a peak as she cried out. Her insides clenched repeatedly, pulsing around him. The part of her mind that watched from above saw flashes of blue, a glow that surrounded their writhing forms as they became one.

~*~

Chris held still as Sarah's orgasm subsided. It took a monumental effort to keep from spilling his seed, but he wanted this moment to last as long as possible. Giving her the best orgasm of her life was his objective, and the look on her face as she shuddered beneath him with the aftermath told him he might have succeeded.

Her breasts were crushed beneath his chest. Her legs were wrapped around his. It didn't get any better than this. A few minutes earlier, he was convinced it was all over, that he'd never see her again. Now he was buried deep inside her and he never wanted to leave.

Moments before she hit her peak, he'd felt as though he was in two places at once. It must have been the crystal's influence, but his mind had done that weird thing again, leaving his body to explore another dimension. But this time, Sarah was there, or her mind was, watching with him as their bodies wrestled as one. No one else would ever understand—they'd think they were both insane. The melding of their psyches together was almost as exquisite as their physical bonding. The mental pleasure was ethereal, almost like a dream, and the physical pleasure was raw and demanding. Together it made for a mind-blowing experience that could not be explained.

Her eyes were open now, deep green and glistening. Her pink lips were swollen from his kisses, and he bent to touch his lips to hers. It was a gentle kiss, followed by a deeper, rougher kiss as the passion built again. Placing his arms under her, he held her to him as he flipped over onto his back. She sat up, and he enjoyed the view. Her long hair, a sandy brown shot through with golden highlights, was tousled, giving her a wild look. Her breasts were firm, the rosy nipples still taut with arousal. He reached up to cup one, causing her to sigh.

It was she who controlled the movement now, leaning forward on her hands and sliding back and forth with her hips. He grabbed onto her butt, squeezing, enjoying the feel of her flesh under his fingers. He closed his eyes to concentrate, and found his mind floating away again. As his mental self watched from above, he saw her leaning over him, her hips finding a rhythm. Sensing her own astral being next to his, they melded into one as their bodies below reached the breaking point.

His orgasm cascaded over him as he pumped into her, his hips pushing up as she pushed down. He heard her cry out and felt her pulsing around him, then she collapsed forward with a groan. His movement slowed as the pleasure ebbed, and his arms and legs went limp. His mind slowly returned to normal as his movements ceased.

The magic of their union was undeniable.

"Holy hell, Sarah. We've still got it."

Laying on top of him, she didn't move. "Oh, yes. Freaking awesome."

Then she rolled off, settling in beside him with her head on his shoulder. She raised her head, looking at his partially limp member, with the condom still in place.

He knew she needed reassurance. "It's alright. Still intact."

Snuggling back in, she laughed softly. "Guess I'm paranoid."

"I understand." He cradled her in his arms, sighing. "This is how it should always be, between us."

Her voice was barely a whisper. "It will be. Nothing will get in our way, ever again. I promise."

"So do I, Sweet. So do I."

17   The Talk

She made it back to work later than promised, but she'd already delegated most of her duties to Martina, so there wasn't anything urgent she'd missed. Which was fortunate, because she was so blissed-out from her time with Chris she had little brain capacity or physical energy for anything else. Martina must have noticed, because she kept grinning at Sarah all afternoon. "What, Martina? Am I missing something?"

Her co-worker shook her head. "I'd say you had a very good lunch. You have the glow of a well-loved woman."

Heat filled her cheeks. Was it that obvious? *Oh, well. It's true.* "I told you, I went to visit Amanda and see the baby."

The other girl's dark eyes sparkled with interest. "And then?"

Sarah looked around, to be sure no one else was nearby. Confident the others in the office were out of earshot, she whispered, "I had to convince my boyfriend not to break up with me. It worked."

"Boyfriend? You mean the tall blond guy I saw you with in the parking lot?"

"No. I mean Chris, the guy I dated in college. He was at the wake, he knew the professor. Anyway, we're back together."

"So have you changed your mind about Arizona?"

The question was a legitimate one, and it had the effect of throwing a cold bucket of water over her still-warm sex glow. The truth was, they hadn't had time to work out all the details yet. All they had figured out was they wanted to be together.

"No, Sophie and I are still going. He's on his way to New York to take care of some business and family matters. We hope he'll be back in time to leave with me to Sedona. If not, he'll have to join me there later."

"Oh. Well I hope it works out. You look happier than I've seen you in a long time."

"Thanks, Martina. Now I better get some work done before the day's over."

As she turned back to her desk, her last conversation with Chris replayed in her mind. After they made love, she was in a hurry to get back to work. While dressing, they had quickly discussed the possibilities. Chris seemed to have figured out the next step, at least.

"I have to get to New York and work things out with my dad. I've been putting him off all week."

"How long will you be there? You know, I never meant to cause any trouble with your family."

"Well, I doubt he'll be happy when I tell him I can't take the job, and that I'm moving to Arizona with no job prospects at all. But that's not your concern. I want to be with you, whatever it takes. As long as you realize, I have nothing left to offer at this point but myself."

She'd thrown her arms around his neck, touched by his honesty. "That's all I need. But I can talk to a recruiter out there, see if they'll at least start looking for something for you."

"That'll help. I have a few copies of my resume, I'll get one for you. And I'll call you tomorrow, 'cause it'll be late tonight when I get there."

He'd kissed her then, a slow kiss full of promise for their future. A future she knew was beginning right then. It was painful to part after such closeness, but she knew he was doing the right thing. "Call me anyway, to let me know you've arrived safe. I don't want to go another day without hearing from you or seeing you."

"Yes, Ma'am. You have my word."

She was going to have a long talk with her daughter that night. Sophie might be only five years old, but she had a way of understanding what was important. Sarah had always put Sophie's needs and desires in front of her own, now she knew taking care of her own needs and wants was also important.

Somehow, she knew in her heart that it would work out well for her daughter, too. They would be a family, and they would all have a home, together. Chris hadn't mentioned marriage specifically, and neither had she. Everything was happening so fast, but at least she knew they were going to be together, for good this time. There would be time to discuss the next step in their relationship once they were settled.

~*~

That evening, she and Sophie ate grilled cheese sandwiches for dinner and packed up some clothes, deciding what they were going to take to wear on the trip. Sophie asked question after question, mostly about the baby but also about life in Arizona. Sarah promised to take her to the hospital the next evening to meet Ryan, unless Zac and Amanda were able to bring him home.

"Momma, I'm going to miss Frodo. And Uncle Zac, Aunt Mandy and baby Ryan, too."

"Honey, you haven't even met the baby."

"But I'll miss him. I wanted to play with him. Like a little brother."

Her heart ached at the thought of leaving her friends, so she understood her daughter's lament. "Sophie, let's go sit on the sofa for a minute." When they were settled on the sofa, Sarah started the conversation she'd been pondering all afternoon. "Sophie, do you like my friend, Mr. Chris?"

Her smile was immediate, as though picturing him in her mind. "Yes. He's nice. He gave me that panda."

"And what about my other friend, Mr. Wes? We went to his party in Denver?"

Her face went blank, then her soft blonde brows knit together. "He seems nice. He has a pretty house. But I don't think you like him."

It was warm in the room but she felt a chill at Sophie's words. How could a child be so intuitive? It reminded her to be careful around her daughter, who observed much more than she let on.

"I do, he's still my friend. In fact..." she hesitated. What good could come of revealing his role now, when they hadn't even figured out what his role would be? Having Chris move in with them was going to be a big adjustment, and she didn't want to pile too much on at once. She should talk to Wes again, and see if he even wanted to be involved. If not, perhaps it would be best to wait until Sophie was older to tell her about her father.

"What, Mamma?"

"Mr. Wes said he will miss us after we leave, and he may come for a visit sometime. Okay?"

"Okay. Will Mr. Chris come visit, too?"

"Remember when I said he used to be my boyfriend, years ago?"

Sophie nodded. "Yes."

"Well, we realized we still love each other, so he's going to be coming with us to Arizona."

The relief of admitting they were in a committed relationship flowed from her solar plexus out through her fingers. It was a palpable feeling, unknotting the tension of resistance that had accompanied every thought of Chris she'd had for the past eight years. The wait was over. No more longing, no lost sleep due to wondering what might have been. That was replaced now with hope, and expectations for all the new memories they would make.

"Okay, Mamma. Can I go play now?"

The five-year old was back, and the old soul that shone through Sophie's eyes now and then was gone, back into her hiding place. *That's it? What was I so worried about?*

"No, it's time for your bath, young lady. Go get your robe and meet me in the bathroom."

As she filled the tub with water, she laughed at herself for her anxieties. Children were adaptable; Sophie would adjust to Chris being around. It might not always be harmonious, but at least now she wouldn't be alone to handle the challenges of raising Sophie. And, who knew? Maybe someday, a little brother or sister would be added to the mix. She smiled at the thought, as Sophie climbed into the tub.

Imagining the future was pleasant, but she still had some loose ends to attend to. Tomorrow, she would call Wes and hopefully come to some agreement. She didn't want to leave things on bad terms with him, though she had to make it clear they were connected by having Sophie in common, and nothing else. Maybe he'd cooled off from his hissy fit the other night enough to think like a mature adult. Maybe.

~*~

Chris woke to the sounds of traffic and sirens, his sluggish brain slowly realizing he was no longer in a hotel in Colorado. His parent's apartment was several stories up, but the sounds of the city were constant. It felt familiar, bringing back memories of growing up amidst the hectic pace of New York City. He looked around as he got out of bed, feeling more accustomed to his surroundings. The apartment was tastefully furnished with antiques and one-of-a-kind pieces. Stately but eclectic, just like his parents.

The alluring scent of coffee led him to the kitchen, where he found his mother reading a newspaper. She looked up at him, and her smile spoke volumes. "There's my baby. I know, you're over thirty now, but you're still my baby."

He leaned over to hug her where she sat, then headed for the coffee pot. "Well, your baby's in a bit of a pickle. I'm not looking forward to my meeting with Dad."

Katherine O'Langley Levine had been managing tussles between her two sons and their father for years. Somehow she managed to not take sides yet maneuvered them into agreeing, even after the worst blow outs. She had a degree in Behavioral Psychology but never practiced, though she had a natural way of helping people work things out. She sometimes volunteered for various organizations, and that kept her skills sharp. Watching her and having many late-night discussions on what motivated people to do the things they do had an impact on Chris. It was one of the reasons he eventually decided to pursue a career in Psychology.

Kath, as her friends called her, had an easygoing approach to life, whereas her husband, Joachim, was all business. Chris had always wondered how they ever got together, or stayed together, as different as they were. But he had come to understand that sometimes people can complement each other, filling needs they never knew they had.

"Chris, just tell him the truth. You know he hates subterfuge. It just makes him wonder what you're not telling him. Once he gets over his emotions, he'll see reason. He always does."

"I know." He knew she was right, but it didn't ease his anxiety much. He sipped at his coffee, and picked up a bagel from the plate on the table. He sniffed it, inhaling the scent of garlic and spices. There were hard rolls, too. He was probably going to gain a few pounds before he left.

Kath put down her paper, and studied him. "So practice on me. What are your plans?"

He had been so tired the night before, arriving by taxi at their apartment. It was past midnight, and though the city was still alive and jumping, he wasn't. He kept to small talk with his parents and then went to bed. He promised to be at his father's office at ten, a few hours from now.

"Mom, it's not at all what he wants to hear. I can't take the job. Something's come up."

Her dark blue eyes narrowed, but a knowing smile graced her lips. "Something or someone?"

His voice was resigned. He was tired of hiding his intentions, and he never could fake it with her, anyway. "Someone. It's Sarah. The one I dated in college, just before graduation."

She reached over the table, and grasped his hand. Hers was soft and warm, comforting. "Do you love her?"

He didn't hesitate; the words came out before he could think of a reaction. "Yes. And I've never stopped, even though we broke up years ago. But we're back together now, and I need to be with her. Whatever that takes."

"Then tell him. Maybe not in those words, but...offer a compromise. He may not accept it, but at least he'll know you are willing to sacrifice for what you want. He'll respect that more than if you just refuse the position."

He pondered her words. Immediately an idea came to mind that just might work. "I'll think of something. But, there's more, Mom. I'm having some financial trouble, so I'm selling my condo. And I'm moving to Arizona to be with Sarah. Like, really soon."

It felt good to tell someone, even though he knew she couldn't solve his problems for him. He trusted her judgement, though, and hoped she'd at least point him in the right direction.

"If you love her, and she loves you, you'll find a way to work things out."

That's it? Love conquers all? What the hell...

He munched on the bagel and finished his coffee. If only it were that easy to solve life's problems. Maybe he'd been alone too long, or with the wrong people too much, to know what it was like to have someone you could work with to face life's battles. That undeniable confidence that no matter what, your partner has your back.

He hoped with all his heart he would have that with Sarah.

He took his dishes to the sink, and stopped to hug his mother on the way back to his room. "Thanks, Mom. Love you."

"Love you, too, baby. You'll work things out. And you know, if you need money, all you have to do is ask."

"I know. But I'll be okay." Taking money from his parents was the last thing he wanted. He had to prove he could do this on his own, take care of his own problems. Though at the moment, he wasn't sure how he was going to pull that off.

Just before ten, he was dressed in a suit and nice shoes, and waiting outside his father's office door. The leather arms of the chair were damp from his sweaty palms, and he adjusted his tie for tenth time. It was his own father, he shouldn't be so nervous. But his plans sounded foolish to his own ears, when he'd rehearsed his speech in the bathroom earlier. Throwing everything away to be with a woman you hadn't seen in years didn't exactly sound like a smart idea.

He was ushered in to his father's office by an assistant, and offered coffee. He declined, and waited patiently while Joachim Levine finished a phone call where he was putting someone quite succinctly in their place. He hung up the phone calmly, and faced his son with what passed, for him, as a smile. Just a small curve at the corner of his mouth, and then his face went serious again.

He was all business this morning, but Chris knew there was love and kindness beneath the hardened exterior. He wasn't a warm and fuzzy sort of dad, but he cared for his children and helped them when they needed it. It was the gauntlet of guilt and hour-long lectures that made finding the warm side of the man so difficult. But Chris knew it was worth it.

"So, Chris. You're finally here. You want to tell me what's really been going on?"

His mother's words echoed back in his mind. He knew there was no easy way to handle this, so he just went for it, hoping for the best.

"I'm really looking forward to working at your company, Dad. From what you told me, it sounds like they've got some great ideas on handling corporate workforce behavioral issues. My experience will fit in with that, and I'm especially interested in developing some testing methods, so I can help them understand how to increase efficiency and improve team building."

Now his father's smile was about as bright as he'd ever seen it, though his eyes showed a touch of doubt. "That's great to hear, Chris. Almost makes me glad you switched your major to psychology. Never thought I'd say that, though."

It had been a blow out to remember, when he changed his major from business to psychology after moving to Colorado,

mostly because he didn't tell his father until after he graduated. "Yeah, well. I guess it worked out. But, as I said, I'm
eager to work on this. I have several ideas for tests and training modules, similar to ones I've developed for my last job.
But I can only do this on a part-time basis as a consultant."

There it was, the gauntlet had been thrown, only this time
it was he who had put the ultimatum on the table. No more
asking his father's permission, or approval. He was an adult,
in charge of his own destiny.

"What? I thought you were on board full time. That's what
you agreed to."

"I did, but my circumstances have changed. I'm moving
to Arizona soon, but I still wanted to contribute in way that
was meaningful and didn't leave you hanging. I can develop
the work there, and using the phone, faxes, and conference
calls, I think it will work. Then I can come here a few times a
year to work with the team, to demonstrate and refine the
methods, if need be."

His father's expression was a mixture of surprise, anger
and pride. Chris had no idea if the proposal would work for
the company, but he had to try. To be honest, he rather liked
the idea. It would give him a measure of freedom and still
allow him to meet his obligations.

"So why Arizona?"

"My girlfriend, Sarah, is moving there, with her daughter.
I want to be with them. I'm going to be with them."

He held his breath. Joachim sat back in his chair looking
at him like a tiger assessing a potential meal. One finger was
across his lips, then he shook his head. Disappointment laced
his voice. "You're doing all this for a girl. I should have
known."

"Yes, you *should* know what it's like to risk everything to
be with the woman you love. I bet it wasn't easy telling your
Jewish parents you were marrying a nice Irish Catholic girl."

The dark eyes lost their predatory look and turned soft,
with a hint of sparkle. "No, it wasn't. I'll give you that. But I

didn't give up my career to do it. I needed to support us. I wasn't in debt and just throwing opportunities away."

He leaned forward in his chair, determined to make his father understand. "Because you didn't have to, Dad, but this is my life. I know I can make things right in time, my finances will improve eventually. But I'll never find another Sarah. We are together again after eight years apart, and I'm not going to let her go now. Not for anything."

They locked eyes for a long moment, then Joachim nodded. "Okay. Let me approach my partners about your proposal and see what they say. I appreciate you looking for a solution, son."

They stood and shook hands, and Chris walked away, his step a little lighter. Maybe there was hope for the future after all.

18 The Commitment

Sarah dropped Sophie off at Peggy's house Friday morning, and headed to her last day of work at the Fort Winston Tourism Office. It had been a second home to her, and she was going to miss her friends and coworkers. Hell, she was going to miss Fort Winston, if she was honest. For so many years it had been a part of her life.

She was surprised to find her cubicle decorated with farewell banners and balloons. At lunch, they had pizza brought in and even a cake. "It's not my birthday," she protested, but they insisted it was a proper send off. She laughed at all the inside jokes and well wishes on the cards several people had given her. Zac had even popped in at lunch to take photos of the festivities. Afterward, she pulled him aside to ask about the baby.

"He's coming home with his mamma tomorrow. Doctor says they're both healthy. We just have to monitor him closely for a while."

She hugged him. "That's great. Sophie's dying to meet him, and to see Amanda, too."

At the end of the day, she was fighting back tears. She said goodbye, leaving work for the last time with a box of her belongings. Her stomach fluttered with a mixture of fear and exhilaration. She'd done it. She'd taken the first step of her new life.

Chris had called late the night before to tell her he'd made it to New York, but hadn't said anything about the meeting with his father. She pushed aside the nagging thought that his parents might talk him out of being with her. Yesterday he sounded so sure, so certain they would be together. She had to cling to that memory until she saw him again.

When she got home, there was a message on her recorder from Wes. *"Sarah, I'm so sorry I yelled at you. Just being stupid and thinking with my you-know-what again. Can I see you tomorrow? Lunch maybe? I just want to make things right before you leave. That's all. Call me."*

It felt all too familiar. It seemed to be his pattern—first he was sweet and funny, then he pushed too far. Then he got mad when he didn't get his way, only to apologize later. Rinse, lather, repeat. If she had to see him on a regular basis it would be stressful, if not outright nerve-wracking. Such behavior would certainly have a negative impact on Sophie, too, if she became closer to Wes than just seeing him as her mother's platonic friend.

There had to be a way to include him in Sophie's life, if that's what he wanted, without having to spend much time with him. When Sophie was older, if she wanted to get to know him better, then it could be arranged. But for now, Wes would have to be content to stay in the background.

She changed into comfortable clothes, and set about making dinner. All that was left in the cupboard was a can of soup, and as it simmered on the stove, she called Wes.

His voice was in pleasant-Wes mode. "Hey, I'm so glad you called back, darlin'. I miss you already."

She couldn't say the same, but kept her tone even. "Thanks. So I can meet you for lunch tomorrow. I'd also like to clear the air about some things before I go."

They made plans to meet at a coffee shop near her house at eleven. She called Peggy to ask her to watch Sophie for a few hours, figuring Zac would have his hands full with Amanda and the baby. She answered as Sarah thought she would. "Sure. She's no problem at all. I'm going to miss having a little girl around."

Another pang of sadness over someone she would miss. The strong connection Amanda had with her family had been a blessing, and they often included Sarah and Sophie, made them feel welcome. Birthdays, holidays, they were always invited to join in. It made not having her own extended family easier to bear. Now she and Chris and Sophie were going to work together to find new traditions and ways to make events special.

The next day she waited for Wes at the appointed place. He was fifteen minutes late, as usual, but she let it slide. He leaned down to kiss her cheek when he arrived and slid into the booth across from her.

"Gorgeous as ever, I see."

She smiled, knowing full well she hadn't taken much care with her appearance, wanting to present her true self to him. Her pony tail and sweatshirt were more suited to cleaning her house, which was what she had planned for the rest of the afternoon. "Thanks, Wes. So what was it you had to say?" She purposely let him start talking, to see what he had in mind.

He ran a hand through his feathered blond hair, and leaned back in his seat. "Well, first I wanted to say I'm sorry for the other night. You're a lady and I was forgetting my manners."

"Fair enough. It had been a long day…but, there's something else on your mind?"

"Yes." He hesitated, as though searching for the right words. "Well, I've been thinking, and I know now it's me who should be honored to have a child with you. You're amazing, Sophie is awesome and I'm also sorry that I missed out on her life up until now."

She was stunned. The urge to pinch herself to see if she was dreaming was interrupted by the waitress who'd come to take their order. She was glad for the momentary diversion so she could formulate an answer. When she did, it was heartfelt. "Wow, Wes. I wasn't sure I'd ever hear you say that."

He actually blushed, and she began to believe he meant it. His voice was low when he spoke, with a touch of regret. "I just never had to think of anyone but myself before, so it took me awhile to get used to the idea."

"So…are you saying you want to be part of Sophie's life?"

He was fidgeting with his fork, then twirling a straw around in his soda glass. She enjoyed his nervousness, to a degree, although she doubted he felt as awkward as she had felt at his parents' house. But it indicated he cared. "Yes, I do. But you're still dead set on leaving, aren't you?"

She nodded, not saying a word to prompt him. He'd already taken more responsibility than she'd expected, so she wanted to see how far he was willing to go.

He cleared his throat and continued. "Have you told her that I'm her father?"

"No, I think she's a bit too young to comprehend all that just yet. Maybe when she's older." Relief crossed his face. So she added, "You're not ready, either. Are you?"

"To be honest, no. I'm not. Maybe that's why I gave you such a hard time. I was trying to prove to you, and to myself that I was ready."

"Well, it takes more than just buying her toys, or taking her to the zoo. Being a parent is the hardest job in the world, but it's also the most rewarding."

"That's why you're so amazing. You did it all on your own. But I want to help, I really do."

Their food arrived and they chatted about other things while they ate. She picked through her salad, her mind spinning. She was glad Wes was being cooperative, but she was still feeling cautious. When he seemed finished with his meal, she brought the conversation back to Sophie. "I'd be glad to write and call occasionally to let you know how she's doing, Wes. Someday, when she's older, if she wants to get to know you, we can talk about it then."

"Fair enough," he said. "I have some money set aside, and I'd like to give you something, just to help get her started. You know, like for school and all that."

"Really? Well, that would certainly help. What did you have in mind?"

"I have ten I can spare. I can send more later, like when I sell stocks or get a bonus or something."

"Ten...thousand?"

"Yep. I know it's not much, and I have some catching up to do."

It was way more than she'd expected of him, and she wondered what he'd want in return. "So, just like that? No strings attached?"

He stared at her as if he'd never seen her before. "Of course not. Just make good on your promise to keep me in the loop, and tell her about me when she's ready. If she wants to spend time with me then, I'll be there."

"Okay. I will. But what about your parents? Have you told them anything?"

She'd worried his parents might try to fight her, do something legal. She liked the idea of Sophie having grandparents, but wanted it to happen in a positive way, not because of a custody battle. She didn't know them well enough to predict what they might do.

"No. I think they'd be happy, but I wanted you and me to work this out on our own. They tend to want to keep control of things, plus, they have plenty of grandkids already to keep them occupied. When Sophie's ready, we can introduce them again."

"Thank you, Wes. That's probably best for now."

He paid for lunch, and as he walked her to her car, she began to relax. He might always be the spoiled rich playboy-type, but underneath all that, he did have a heart. She hugged him, promising to call when they reached Sedona. His face changed when she mentioned her trip.

"He's going with you, isn't he?"

"Yes. Does that bother you?"

"I'd be lying if I said no. But I knew he was yours, and you were his, that day at the wake. There was this...connection."

She placed a hand on his cheek. "Take care of yourself, Wes Porter."

"You take care of yourself, and my girl."

They smiled at each other, and she sensed a genuine connection with him, for the first time. She hoped it wasn't the last.

~*~

Chris picked up the phone and dialed Sarah's number. It was Saturday evening, and he was in the process of packing his freshly laundered clothes into his suitcase. He wondered when he was going to be able to stop living out of his case and finally be settled.

His heart skipped a beat when he heard her voice. He missed her more than he ever had. Having had a taste of how good it was to be with her in every way possible caused a craving that wouldn't let up. It would only be quelled by seeing her, but talking on the phone was the next best thing. They chatted for a few minutes, then he couldn't wait any longer to tell her his good news. "So, my dad's company agreed to my proposal, on a trial basis, anyway. But that means I'll be able to work for them remotely while I'm looking for permanent work in Sedona. I just have to come back here for meetings every once in a while."

"That's great. I'm sure we can work that out. I faxed your resume to a recruiter yesterday, when I was still at the office. My new boss Nadine recommended him. He called back right away and said he thought you'd be a great fit to work at this new Learning Center, where they teach mediation and all sorts of cool stuff. He's going to talk to them about it. And it's close to these apartments I want to look at."

"Thanks, Sweet, seems like everything's falling into place. But guess what else happened?" He was enjoying himself, leading her along. It had been so long since he'd had good news to share.

"You won the New York lottery?"

"No. I called my realtor a few hours ago and she told me we have an offer on my condo."

"That's totally awesome, babe. I'm so happy for you."

"Yeah. It looks like maybe my luck has finally turned. If the sale goes through, I'll have to go back to California sometime after we get to Sedona. But it won't take long, I don't think. Anyway, I can't wait to see you. I have a flight early tomorrow morning so I should be at your place about noon."

"Really? That's fantastic. I can't wait, either. I miss you."

Then she told him about the baby being home, and how Sophie was doting on him as though he were her little brother. They planned to spend a few days cleaning the house, renting the trailer and packing it up. If all went well, they would leave by Wednesday morning for Sedona.

Talking only made him miss her more, so they said good night and he went back to packing. It had felt good to end the conversation with, "I love you", and to hear it back. He planned to tell her so every day. With Teressa, and some of the others he'd dated, he hadn't said it often, if he did at all. Back then he'd believed that saying those words in a routine manner devalued the sentiment, but now he couldn't imagine a time when he would ever say those words to Sarah and not fully mean them. Whether he said it once or one thousand times in a day, it would be sincere.

Later, having a glass wine with his parents in the living room, he reveled in a feeling of contentment. There was still much work to do, and he knew his struggles weren't over. The difference was, he now had hope, and someone to fall back on. It was also the first time he truly felt like a responsible adult in his parents' eyes, and he realized he was going to miss them, too. He raised his glass in a toast.

"Mom, Dad, I can't thank you enough for your under-standing and support. I know it hasn't always been easy put-ting up with me." He grinned at the way they glanced at each other, no doubt recalling the many times he'd tried their pa-tience, even broke their hearts. He also saw how quickly their expressions turned to pride. "But I know that from here on out, I'm going to make you proud. I know who I am, what I'm capable of, and where I want to be. Most importantly, who I want to be with."

Sitting on the sofa opposite Chris, Kath and Joachim both raised their glasses, murmuring, "Mazel Tov". Then Joachim set down his glass, and reached over for his wife's hand.

"Chris, your mother and I have always been proud of you, and your brother. Even though you both sometimes went off track, you'd always find a way to do the right thing in the end. That's all a parent can hope for."

Kath's warm voice chimed in. "You'll find that out soon enough, when you have kids of your own."

It hit him then he was about to take on a new role, being around Sophie. Maybe someday soon, he'd be a stepfather? The thought pleased him, more than he expected. "I hope so, Mom. I think I'm looking forward to it, actually. When you meet Sophie, you'll understand. She's a special little girl."

"Well, then. Looks like we're going to have to take a trip to Arizona sometime, Kath," Joachim said, reaching for the bottle to pour them all some more wine. "Here's to meeting your new family, Chris. And seeing your new home."

As they raised their glasses, Chris had to fight back a lump in his throat to swallow the wine. Emotions he'd never felt before were taking over, and he was honored to feel them. Love. A sense of commitment. A willingness to sacrifice for and to protect those he loved. It was more important than any possession, or any career accomplishment. He now had someone—no, two someones-to come home to.

That's where he was going—home. Anywhere he was with Sarah, and their new family, was home.

He couldn't be happier.

Epilogue
The Higher Elevation

Sarah put her overnight bag in the back seat, leaving room for Sophie. A pillow and blanket, several books and Sophie's favorite toy, the stuffed Pink Panther Wes had given her, were also in the backseat in preparation for the drive to Sedona. It was only about twelve hours, including stops, but Sophie had never been in the car that long before, so she wanted to make her as comfortable as possible.

"We ought to get to Nadine's place by eight or nine," she explained to Sophie as she closed the door to their house for the last time. "It's going to be a long drive, but you can take a nap if you get sleepy. Now, go and say goodbye."

She blinked back a tear as she followed her daughter to where Zac and Amanda were standing on the sidewalk. Ryan was in Amanda's arms, wiggling and moving his chubby little hands about. Sarah looked up at Zac, and saw the face of a proud new father. "You better send us pictures of him, Zac. I know you're going to take a bunch, so you can surely spare a few."

Amanda laughed, and elbowed her husband. "He's gone through two rolls of film already."

He shrugged his shoulders in response. "Can you blame me? He's the most beautiful baby that ever lived."

Sarah smiled, thinking he wasn't far off. "He is beautiful. Good thing he takes after his mamma then."

Zac rolled his eyes, and she knew she was going to miss sparring with him. She moved forward, and he held her in a long bear hug. "Call us when you get there, okay? I don't care how late."

She promised she would. She side-hugged Amanda, careful not to disturb Ryan. Sophie was on tiptoe, trying to get a better look at the baby. Chris came over to join them, picking her up so she could see Ryan and plant a kiss on his head. "Trailer's locked and the hitch is secured. I guess we're all set." He set Sophie down, and extended a hand to Zac. "Thanks for everything, man. We'll keep you posted."

"You better." He shook Chris's hand, turning it into a loose guy-hug, both men slapping each other on the back. After he pulled away, he warned, "And don't you two go and elope. I promised Sarah years ago I'd shoot her wedding photos. I'd hate to miss out on that job."

Chris shot her a look, and she felt her cheeks go pink. But the light in his eyes told her he liked the idea as much as she did. He moved close, taking her hand. Then he spoke the very words she was thinking, surprising her and causing a flutter of joy in her stomach. "You'll both be the first to know when we get engaged. Besides Sophie, of course."

Zac smiled, leaning down to hug Sophie. "Frodo's going to miss you, and we will, too."

Sophie's smile faded and her cheeks turned bright pink, as tears began to form. She hiccupped and started to cry. "I don't want to go."

Sarah picked her up, patting her back. "Shhh…it's alright. We'll come back for a visit soon."

Chris held up his hand, and walked to the car. He returned a moment later, carrying something brown and fuzzy. "Sophie…this is for you."

At his voice, she turned from Sarah's shoulder to see. He held out a stuffed brown puppy, and the resemblance to Frodo was close enough to catch her attention.

Zac jumped in. "Hey, he looks just like Frodo. Now you have your own puppy."

Sophie sniffed and reached out for the toy, holding it to her. Sarah set her down on the grass. "What do you say, Sophie?"

She stood quietly for a moment, then looked at Chris. "Thank you."

Chris leaned down, and ruffled her hair. "You're welcome. I saw him at the airport gift shop and knew you'd like him."

Something in Sarah's heart clicked, and she knew things were going to work out just fine.

Amanda's eyes were tearing up now, too, and she handed the baby to Zac. Hugging Sarah tight, she whispered in her ear, "Anytime you need to talk, just call. Promise?"

"I will." A tear slipped out, and Sarah pulled from the embrace, wiping her cheek. "Okay, let's go, before I change my mind."

As they pulled away from the curb, she looked back at Sophie, who was already engrossed in one of her picture books, holding her stuffed puppy tight. Chris was driving, and he reached for her hand, saying, "We'll see them again soon. It's not the end of the earth, you know. Just a few hours away."

"I know. I'll miss them for sure. But I'm excited to start our new life together."

He kissed the back of her hand, still entwined in his. "Me too. Undeniably so."

Undeniable. That's what their love was. From the first time she saw him, years earlier, their connection was an unexplainable phenomenon, something born on a higher elevation. Somehow she knew it would always be so. She sat back in her seat, looking out at the road ahead, ready for anything—as long as they were together.

The End

About the Author

A lifelong entrepreneur, Renee Regent spent most of her life writing for business. But she never lost her love of writing stories, especially romance, science fiction, and fantasy. She's always been fascinated with the science of how the universe works, but equally entranced by the unexplained. Being an incurable romantic, she now writes stories about the power of love, with a supernatural twist. Her stories feature psychics, witches, ghosts and ordinary people who do extraordinary things.

Renee, a California native, lives in Atlanta with her husband, three cats and four turtles. When not working or writing, she can be found sitting on her deck enjoying nature. Wine may or may not be involved....

A member of Georgia Romance Writers and the Georgia Writer's Association, Renee also loves blogging and sharing her ideas on the business side of being an author, trends in fiction, and tips she has learned in her writing journey.

Now Available
Unexplained (Higher Elevation Series Book One)
Untouched (Higher Elevation Series Book Two)

Thanks for reading! Honest reviews are always appreciated.

If you would like more information, stop by my website at http://reneeregent.com for news on upcoming releases, blog posts, special events, social media links, and to sign up for my newsletter. Subscribers are eligible for giveaways and special items not available to the public.

Made in the USA
Charleston, SC
20 January 2017